Lucy's Gift

Allysan Redwell

I hope you can 'paws' for a moment to enjoy a 'tail' of two rescues.

Printed in the United States of America.

LUCY'S GIFT by Allysan Redwell

LUCY'S GIFT is an original publication. This work has never before appeared in book form. Lucy and Rascal, my two rescues, are the inspiration for the writing of this story.This is a work of fiction. With the exception of Lucy and Rascal, all characters are fictional, however, the story is based on my experience with a local rescue organization. Permissions have been received for characters whose lives are fictionally portrayed, yet based on factual circumstances.

My purpose in the writing of this novel, is to give insight into the plight of surrendered animals and the hope that they can find when individuals are willing to open their hearts to the idea of adoption.

ISBN: 9781688574991

Cover photo courtesy of Susan Sterritt.

For my 'children' and grand-children; you are my blessed reasons for living.

For my Lord; you are my inspiration and the reason for loving my life.

If you are interested in adopting a pet, please contact local animal shelters or rescue organizations in your area.

If you live in Colorado and are interested in adopting a rescue dog, please contact:

The Misfits Dog Rescue

217 Garden Dr. Penrose, CO 81240

Or online at: www.doggyheroes.com

You may contact their Misfit Crusader, Susan Sterritt, at: misfitsdr@gmail.com

National Mill Dog Rescue, Peyton, CO is an organization that rescues and rehabilitates dogs that have come from commercial puppy mills. They can be found online at: www.milldogrescue.org

Chapter One

The moment she heard the hall closet door being opened, the little black dog came running down the stairs as fast as her short legs could carry her. As she watched her master take his coat off the hanger, she began to yip and dance around at his feet.

"Yes, Lucy, you'll be going with me this morning. We have to make a quick trip to the lawyer's to sign some papers." The elderly man smiled as his little dog sat momentarily, her tail wagging in a circle as fast as it could possibly go. "Once we're done there, you and I will go for a nice walk around the lake."

Lucy looked adoringly up at him with her big, brown eyes, seeming to smile from the joy she felt as she looked into the face of her master. As he reached for her leash, she was unable to contain her excitement at the thought of going bye-bye and she rose up onto her back feet, holding her front paws up towards him. She continued to stand on her hind legs even as he snapped the Italian leather leash onto the leather and diamond studded black collar that she wore around her neck. With the leash in place, he reached down to give her soft little head a scratch behind the ears.

"Oh Lucy, what would I do without your happy little presence to greet me and keep me company every day? I'm afraid I'd be so terribly lost without you."

Lucy gave a gentle little whine, as if to say she didn't know what he would do, either. She watched his every move as he sat down onto the oak bench in order to remove his slippers so he could slide his feet into his shoes.

"I'm not going to put a jacket on you this morning since we're having such a nice fall day. It's much warmer than what we usually see during the first week of November, isn't it little girl? Maybe our warm Indian summer will be able to take us all the way to Thanksgiving, at least. But in December, I want another of our white Christmas's." he said as he bent over and began to tie his shoes.

Lucy once again rose up onto her hind feet, holding her paws high, signaling that she wanted him to pick her up.

"Be patient little dog, I'm not quite ready to head out the door, I still need to tie my shoes and then I want a moment to catch my breath."

Lucy replied with another soft whine. Since patience wasn't one of the traits that she seemed to have acquired, she stood again, on her back feet with little paws lifted high.

He couldn't help but smile at her, as her stance reminded him of his children when they had been toddlers. He thought of all the times, when they were first learning to walk, how they would reach their hands high and wanted to be picked up by their daddy. His son, and a few years later, his daughter, had been the joy of his life when they were young. He and Julie, his precious wife, had been so elated to finally become parents after waiting for more than ten years after they had become man and wife. They had been forced to learn the meaning of the word patience as they had longingly waited for parenthood.

Those had been wonderful times, the days before his business had grown to immense proportions and begun to demand so much of his time. As their wealth had increased, he and Julie had made the mistake of lavishing every imaginable luxury on their children. It had been his way of trying to make up for all the hours he'd had to put in at work, necessitating an absence from his family. In their early years, as a young married couple, he and Julie had been through so many difficult times; often wondering as they had looked back, how they had ever managed to get by.

He surmised that his children weren't entirely to blame for their 'entitlement' attitudes.

It had been so much fun to provide them with everything that he had never had. His own father had suddenly left when he was a teen, and he'd worked an after school job in order to help his mother make ends meet for he and his younger sister. When the opportunity to attend college had presented itself through the hard work of a dedicated school counselor, committed to helping him to find every grant and scholarship available, he had followed through and had graduated with impeccable grades.

He had chosen wisely and gone into the world of financial planning. The bear and bull markets were thrilling to him, as he'd advised his clients with the wisdom that came so naturally. He had taken some of those very recommendations to heart and gone on to eventually start his own investment firm. He and Julie had always tried to keep their eyes on the past, remembering what it was like to scrape for every dime. Their increased status had necessitated that they live in a much larger home than they had ever imagined, enabling the entertaining that went along with wealth. But even then, they had maintained a home within reason, not nearly as lavish as many of his clients maintained. He was determined to embrace his roots and was well known for his humble integrity. He was deeply trusted and as a result, had been highly successful throughout his career.

His Julie had been the light of his life ever since meeting during their college years. He remembered the first time that he had ever seen her. He was working part time as a chef at a popular restaurant near the college. She had been hired as a waitress and he smiled as he thought about the day she had walked in, wearing the cotton dress that was the required uniform for all of the waitresses. She was so petite that she had looked like a young girl who had decided to play dress up, in a gown that belonged to her mother. From the moment he had laid eyes on her, he'd told the other cook standing beside him that he was determined to one day, make her his wife. Unfortunately, Julie hadn't felt the same way upon meeting him. It had taken awhile to build a friendship, but eventually, his gentle kindness had slowly won her heart and they had married one month after graduating from college.

Julie had supported him in every way throughout the many wonderful years that they had been together. She had remained the love of his life until the day had come when a failing heart had claimed her life. Even now, years later, the sense of loss had remained. Lucy had been a gift from Julie in the early days of learning about her diagnosis. He knew that she had been thinking ahead in case anything happened, knowing that she hadn't wanted him to be alone.

Because their son and daughter had both received the best of everything as they had grown, being privileged had not fostered the kind of character that he had hoped he would have seen in his offspring. Money had spoiled them in their younger years, and even though he and Julie had required that they take time from their studies to volunteer by serving the less privileged, their character traits had been sorely lacking throughout their lives. Neither his son nor his daughter had gone into careers like his, or careers that had amounted to much of anything, for that matter. They had both squandered the trust funds that had been established for them at birth. The monies should have taken them well into their adult lives, but instead, it had been wasted on expensive sport cars, designer clothing, expensive handbags and every other imaginable thing that their hearts had desired.

As their children had advanced into their 30's, he and Julie had finally been forced to say 'no' to their constant requests for hand-outs, having decided that it would be for their best interests. They had hoped that it would foster a growth in responsibility. But from that day forward, their adult 'children' hadn't bothered to make any time to spend with him or Julie any longer. They saw them briefly each Christmas, when their son and daughter traveled into town to party with their old friends from school. Their son had been married twice, but neither of the marriages had lasted for more than a few years. Their daughter had married only once and when it had failed, she'd made the decision to remain single like so many of her friends.

He had hoped that their relationships with their parents would have improved when they were informed of their mother's diagnosis. He had longed for them to make the time to spend with Julie during her final months, as her weakened heart began to give out. Sadly, he had been deeply disappointed as they had each made brief visits, more out of duty, than love. He didn't understand how they both could have been so cold-hearted towards their mother, yet he had given them the benefit of a doubt, hoping that it was because they didn't want to face the truth of one day, possibly losing their mother. He had even dared to hope that they might reach out to him in his grief after their mother was gone but that hope was to no avail as, once again, his adult children had seemed to think only of themselves.

Lucy had been a refreshing infusion of light into his and Julie's lives and the little dog had spent every opportunity to be at their feet for every household event. Julie was sure that Lucy thought she was the furry household matriarch and nothing happened without her presence and approval. It was hard to believe that little Lucy was already almost ten years old and that he and his little curly haired dog had been without Julie for the past seven years. Lucy had been there for him and had remained at his side, as a faithful companion, ready to make him laugh with all of her silly antics.

Another soft whine and gentle tap by a furry paw on his knee brought him out of his reverie.

"Yes, little girl, I know…I'm taking much too long and patience is definitely not one of your stronger virtues."

Lucy yipped in agreement, hopped down onto all fours and headed for the front door, with her beloved master in tow.

Chapter Two

"Tyler…Ali! C'mon kids, we're going to be late if we're not out in the car in the next sixty seconds!"

Jamie heard the loud tramping of feet as her two children came running down the stairs from their bedrooms upstairs. As they grabbed their coats off the hooks next to the front door, she handed each of them their lunches and pulled the door shut behind them as they all headed for the car.

"Mom, don't forget that I'll be walking to the rescue right after school, so you won't need to pick me up until five thirty." Ali said as she buckled herself in.

"And don't forget," Ty quickly added, "that I have football practice after school today, so I'll walk over to the high school as soon as I'm done."

"Thanks for the reminders." Jamie said as she finished pulling out of the driveway and onto the street.

She glanced quickly at the clock on the dash of the car, thankful that the predicted snow had held off so she wasn't battling icy streets as she drove somewhat faster than her normal speed. Winter was well on its way and would be depositing plenty of snow during the month of November, if it was anything like the year before.

Was it last year when we already had snow by the time November had arrived? she thought to herself. She couldn't clearly remember many of the details surrounding this time last year. She could hardly believe that more than a year had already passed since one word, cancer, had changed everything in their world.

Her husband, Matt, had begun to complain of a stiff neck and a headache. He had felt sure that it was being caused by nothing more than the new pillow that they had recently purchased. Within weeks, the headache refused to ease up and when he'd suddenly developed paralysis in his left eye, it had marked the beginning of a myriad of tests and a variety of doctors who weren't sure what was causing the problem.

Within a few weeks, Matt's neck, and additionally his back, had become so painful that he'd begun to have problems walking. He had finally been admitted to the hospital after another a scan of his spine had revealed a mass inside the spinal cord. She remembered how much they had hoped that the removal of the mass would solve all of his problems and that he would be on the road to recovery in no time. Unfortunately, as the mass had been evaluated by multiple high profile pathology labs, they had all reached the same consensus. The mass was cancerous and not only was his central nervous system filled with the destructive cells, he also had cancer throughout his body.

His oncologist had seemed deeply discouraged as she had delivered the news. The cancer was so rare that there weren't really any viable treatment options available and the prognosis had been terminal. Six weeks after they had received the diagnosis, Matt had lost his battle to a relentless disease that had shown no mercy. Thankfully, he had been discharged from the hospital and had finished out his final days in the comfort of home, surrounded by the family who loved him.

Jamie swallowed the lump in her throat, attempting to prevent the tears that had so readily found their way down her cheeks in the past year. She was determined to remain dry-eyed, at least until she had finished dropping her children off at the middle school that they both attended. Ali was now an eighth grader and this had been Tyler's first year in middle school. She was so glad that they were back together in school once again. They had needed the encouragement of one another as they had begun the school year without their father's encouragement and participation.

"Mom…Mom! We're here! Are you going to pull over and let us out?" Tyler asked as he softly patted her on the shoulder from the back seat of the car.

"Oh, wow, I'm so sorry. I don't know where my head was! I've always said that I sure am glad that God made necks, or *my* head would be missing!" she replied as she pulled up to the curb and slowed the car to a stop.

Ali looked over at her, the knowing look on her face revealing that she knew where her mother's thoughts had been. "Love you, Mom," Ali said, pausing momentarily, as she reached for her book bag before exiting the car. "Remember, I'll be at the shelter until five thirty."

"Love you, too, Mom." said Ty, as he quickly hugged her good-by before running off to catch up with his friends.

While Jamie watched her children walk through the doors of their middle school, a smile gently tugged at the corners of her mouth. Though they were siblings, she noted the stark differences between the two. Their slender builds were the only similarity. Alison's thick blonde hair and blue eyes reminded Jamie of herself when she was young, but she wondered if Ali's hair would remain blonde, or turn the same caramel color as her own. Alison currently stood a head taller than her younger brother, but Jamie knew that wouldn't last for long, as Ty rapidly approached puberty and the growth spurt that would surely take place before too long. She felt sure that Ty was going to be tall, like his father had been. His dark, almost black hair and dark eyes were just like his dad's and his eyes were framed with long, curly eyelashes and thick, dark eyebrows, just like Matt's. It was bittersweet whenever she looked into Ty's face, as it brought back memories of the man whose resemblance he bore. Alison had often been jealous of her brother's eyelashes. Hers, also, were long and curly, but they were light in color, the same color as her eyebrows. She had often asked why it was that the guys always got the nicest lashes. Jamie had never had an answer for her, because she had often wondered the very same thing.

As Jamie slowly pulled back into traffic and headed for her job at the high school where she taught English, she breathed a sigh. She was so proud of her children. They had stood beside her in the days after Matt had died. Somehow, they had even managed to get through that first Christmas without their dad, after having said the final goodbye just weeks before the blessed holiday had arrived. Jamie couldn't remember if they had even put up the tree that year. She could barely recall any details from the first months after Matt's death. Jamie did remember that there had been many days when her children had returned home from school to find that she had been unable to get dressed, not to mention, prepare a meal. The two of them had worked together in those early months of grief, often preparing simple evening meals for the three of them to eat. When Jamie had felt like she couldn't go on, one look into the faces of her children had prevented her from doing anything foolish and given her the courage to face another day.

As she pulled into the parking lot at school, she dropped her head onto the steering wheel, softly banging it as she asked, "Why? Why? It wasn't supposed to be this way. We were supposed to watch our children grow up, go to college…get married…we were supposed to grow old together! We never got to celebrate a second honeymoon for our twentieth anniversary…an anniversary that was never reached! We had so many plans, plans that we had put together while we were still in college…I want my life back the way it used to be, Matt. I want you back." Heaving a deep sigh, Jamie picked her purse up from the seat beside her, collected herself and headed into the school to begin her day, despite the ongoing pain of her grief.

Chapter Three

"Well then John, are you sure this includes all of the changes to your will that you wanted to have Travis take care of for you?" asked David, a good friend whose companionship dated back to their college years. "I must say, I'm surprised that this is what you had in mind when you made this appointment to meet with me…not totally surprised, mind you, but had no idea what your plans were going to be when I took your call last week when I was filling in for Travis."

"Dave, I've been thinking about this for a long time, now. It's not like I just woke up one morning and made these decisions. These things have been in the works, at least in my mind, for a couple of years. Julie and I had set so many things in place regarding our estate, but these final decisions were mine and mine alone. I know that Julie would have fully approved. I just wanted to be sure that our wealth could bring about some positive changes…changes for the better…hopefully."

He looked down as Lucy lay dozing at his feet. She had been good, really quiet for a change. She always managed to get a little vocal when John's attentions were focused elsewhere. She seemed, almost, to want to join in the conversations that were taking place around her. This time, it was as if she had sensed that this was important business that he had been attending to and she had settled onto the floor next to John's chair. It hadn't taken long before she'd dozed off and had proceeded to let out some soft little snoring sounds as she lay sleeping at her master's feet.

"How are you and Mary doing these days? Are you two still playing golf?" John asked.

"We're both doing great and we manage to get out on the course as often as the weather allows. And as often as our energy allows…which amounts to about once a week. I still remember back when we were trying to teach the 'girls' about the game of golf. Remember? We had finally given up and they had taken the initiative to get 'real' golf lessons, from a 'professional'.

"Oh, I well remember, my friend! It was actually a really good idea because their skills increased enough that it made playing as a foursome much more enjoyable. And do you remember the shock on all of our faces when we went out and Julie whacked her ball, with the wrong club no less, and ended up with a hole in one?"

"I'll never forget that day! The look on her face was priceless!"

"The look on *her* face? What about the looks on *all* of our faces? Your mouth almost dropped to your feet because you still lacked that accomplishment! I almost died laughing after we had all wandered around everywhere, looking for that missing ball and then your dear wife decided to take a look in the hole…and found it! Those were such wonderful times and oh, how thankful I am for the years that we all had together."

"And John, do you remember that time we all bought a set of those expensive knives from that college kid who was trying to supplement his income for school?"

"How could I ever forget? We were all finally getting our businesses established and we finally had some money to spend on those pricey knife sets. We felt that it was for a good cause, knowing how important we felt about kids getting a college education. Remember how he really stressed that every component of the knives had been made in America."

"Oh yes, I do. And how about the day when the knives needed sharpening and we'd decided to get together to have the company rep come to do both sets at our place, in order to 'kill two birds with one stone'?"

John broke into laughter, "Oh my gosh, yes. That little Asian gal showed up…she was extremely proficient at her job and had thoroughly impressed all of us. And then, just before leaving, she turned to us and said, 'Remember, these knives were made in America, but your knife *sharpener*, she is not. She was made in China'."

"Her response caught us all off guard and we about died laughing! Aw, those were the days, my friend."

"Yes, they were Dave, and I wouldn't trade the memories that we've made during our years together, for all the tea in China!" John said with a wink.

"Please remember, John, that our door is always open for you to come and spend time with us. You do know that you're always welcome, don't you?" David asked.

"Definitely. I'll try to get a little better about coming around; now that I'm retired, I won't have any excuses."

"Speaking of retirement, how's it going for you? Any regrets?"

"I feel so relaxed these days, ever since I made the decision to *fully* retire! I've had so much more energy now that I'm not trying to give guidance to clients who think that they know what's best, only to call me up in a panic whenever the market hiccups! And little Lucy is a continual infusion of life on those days when I think I'm too tired to do much of anything. Even though she's almost ten, she just keeps on going and going."

"She sounds a lot like the Energizer Bunny that we see advertised, and that's probably a good thing for an old guy like you." David said with a smirk on his face.

"Look who's talking, my friend. I see only gray hairs in that beard of yours and the top of your head looks just like mine…a little less hair and a lot more gray!"

"So what else are you doing for fun these days…I mean, besides hanging out with Lucy?"

"Hanging out with Lucy seems to be the majority of it. Per usual, she seems to think that we're preparing for a marathon." John said, with a wink, "Or a very slow 1-k, at the very least."

"I hope that she's keeping you in check and you're not pushing yourself too hard. After all, we're both turning 75 in another few months." Dave said, as he stroked the neatly trimmed beard on his face.

"Actually, she and I take a couple of short walks every day. And even though Lucy *is* almost 70 in dog years, she can run circles around this old guy! The walking has been good for both of us and she lives for our morning and afternoon walks, barring aberrant weather conditions. I've definitely become a fair weather walker, now that I've gotten older. I have no desire to take a fall on the ice once the snow begins to fall." John said as he looked down at his little black companion, "Thankfully the ice never stays put for long at this altitude, so we don't end up missing too very many days, even during the winter months. And now, my friend, I've kept you long enough and I want to say thank you for taking this time to meet with me. I deeply appreciate it. Especially since you're finally retired so I assume that you want to get back to doing nothing." John chuckled. "It means a lot to me that you came into the office for this appointment that I had originally made with Travis."

"Not a problem at all," David replied, "And it's been more than just a few years since I retired. And having a son who wanted to step into my place made the transition go really smoothly. It's hard to believe that it's almost ten years now…seems like yesterday! Where does the time go? How did we get to be three quarters of a century old already? Didn't we just graduate from college?" David chuckled.

"If the young had any idea how quickly life will pass them by, maybe they'd make better decisions as they trudge through their lives. I'm definitely thinking of my own children in this situation. How did Travis escape the entitlement trap that my John Jr. and Emily are so caught up in? What did you and Mary do differently?" John asked.

"I think that it came from his time spent in the Army. I still remember how upset Mary and I were when he came home after two years in college and told us that he had decided to put school on hold because he had enlisted. In fact we were more than a little upset. I don't think that I've ever seen Mary come so unglued. Gone was her soft spoken, usually gentle personality. She had really given that son of ours a piece of her mind! And then, when he re-enlisted for another two years after becoming an officer, she wasn't quite as upset, but she still felt really frustrated with him. His days spent serving his country helped him to grow up and it had helped him develop into such a responsible young man, that we realized that his plan had actually been the best one for him." Dave thoughtfully replied, "Travis has always tried to be more than what we ever asked of him. It's as if he's trying to live for some of the young men who didn't have the privilege of making it home. And even after all these years, he continues to stay in touch with some of the families of those who were lost."

"I am *so* deeply appreciative of his service to our country on my behalf. But I'm sure that it was really hard as a parent, to know that your son was spending time in such dangerous places. It's got to be a parent's worst nightmare, knowing that their son or daughter might not come home. What would we do without the young men and women who serve? They're the backbone of America's freedom."

"I agree; and Mary and I ended up being so proud of his service that we regretted our initial response to his decision. There are still times when I reflect back on those days, glad that they're over, yet valuing the character it helped to build in our son. And everything turned out okay, especially since he went back to school after his army days and decided to follow in his old man's footsteps! And, speaking of Travis, he asked me to pass his regrets along for having to miss this meeting today. Since he's not here, I want you to answer this next question perfectly honestly…has my son been living up to your expectations as your legal counsel?"

"That, and then some, my friend. He's almost as good as his old man when it comes to managing my affairs!" John replied with a wink, while giving his gray head an affirmative shake.

"I don't think I'd be calling anyone an old man, especially since you'll hit the next age increase a few weeks before I do!" David replied with a grin, as Lucy awakened and sprung to life with a little yip. "Well then, it looks like your little furry princess is summoning you to leave."

"There's no such thing as patience, when it comes to Lucy. I think she orders me around way more than Julie ever did!" John said, as he reached down to clip Lucy's leash onto her collar. He paused in mid-move and then rolled his left shoulder forward as he rubbed it with his right hand. "Augh, this shoulder is beginning to give me some problems again!"

"Have you gone back in to see your orthopedic doc about it?" David asked.

"Not yet, I just made the call last week and you know how hard it is to get an appointment with a specialist...any specialist! It takes weeks. I finally have an appointment coming up near the end of the month. I'm really hoping that some physical therapy will get it back into shape. I'm definitely not interested in another shoulder surgery. One shoulder surgery was enough...much too painful to ever want to do that again...especially without Julie here to oversee my recovery as she did in the past."

"And wait on you hand and foot?"

"Absolutely, how could I have whined my way through all that pain without someone to dote on my every need?" John laughed.

As soon as he leaned down to clip the leash onto Lucy's collar, she sprang into action, vocally letting both men know that she had been patient enough for all the time that her little body could stand.

"Well, old buddy, if you do need more surgery, just remember, Mary and I are only a phone call away." David said, rising to his feet and reaching out to grasp the hand of his friend.

As John took David's hand, they shook first and then leaned into one another for a friendly embrace, like they had shared so many times before.

"As soon as everything has been filed, I'll have Travis shoot you an email or a text to let you know."

"Thanks, Dave. You, and now Travis, have taken care of things for me for so many years and I deeply appreciate all that you've done." John said, as he opened the office door and followed his little black bundle of yipping energy out the door.

Chapter Four

As John and Lucy rounded the turn in the park near their home, he was once again struck by the beauty of the sun shining on Elk Creek Lake. The late afternoon rays reflected off the water's smooth surface, causing beams of light to dance on some of the branches of the pine trees that stood majestically on the shore. He thoroughly enjoyed the pungent smell of pine as he and Lucy took their daily walks. It was one odor that he was sure he would never tire of inhaling.

He had always enjoyed living in this beautiful community, located a short distance from the panorama of the Rocky Mountains. There were two things that had always fascinated him by virtue of their vastness. One had always been the mountains, feeling that their presence spoke highly of God's majesty. His second fascination had been the ocean. He had never gotten over marveling at the power of the crashing waves, as he had watched the white caps spread as far towards the horizon as he could see. When he had finished grad school, he and Julie had vacillated between choosing a mountainous community for establishing themselves in or a community somewhere near the ocean. The mountains had finally won out and neither of them ever had any regrets about the choice that they had made.

Ah, how I love living here. John had always felt like God had put in some overtime when he had made the range that he felt privileged to gaze upon each and every day. It was almost as if the mountains reached out to lovingly nestle their community in the strength of their rocky arms. He had never tired of arising each morning to look and see how much snow had topped the peaks from any storms that might have passed during the night, while he drank his morning cup of coffee on the porch that faced the panoramic view.

It had always been easy to recognize when a front was moving in, just by looking to the west. Storms were easily seen as they came across the rocky peaks. At times, the peaks helped to divert the brewing storms, dividing them in two, causing them to spread to the north and the south, missing the community completely. Yet, there were other times when storms picked up power as they passed over the high altitude terrain, rapidly cooling the clouds and causing them to dump massive amounts of snow or rain in a short period of time. Although he preferred the sunny, warm days that were sprinkled throughout the winter months, every so often, a massive blizzard was just what everyone needed.

It usually resulted in shutting everything down for a period of a few days. Kids were ecstatic as the list of school closings were announced, one after another, by the anchor men and women who kept everyone well informed. Because of the usual temperate winter climate, it was difficult for the city to keep up with snow removal during a sudden blizzard, due to a lack of equipment. It was during the most severe weather that the citizens banded together, helping one another to shovel drives and walkways. Individuals who owned four wheel drive vehicles were there to lend a hand by helping to transport individuals who had been caught in emergency situations.

He was always amazed at how well mankind came together during times of tragedy and need and had often wished that the acts of kindness would continue on indefinitely. He shook his head as he thought about how quickly everyone went 'back to business' after the need had passed, and continued on with their lives, going back to pulling into their garages and quickly closing their doors. It was almost as if they didn't want to allow enough time for the neighbors whom they had previously spent time together with, shoveling and talking, to enter back into their lives. The world was rapidly becoming such a different place from the one that he had grown up in. No man is an island, but it had begun to seem like individuals really wished that they could be.

Lucy softly whined and sat down to watch as a deer and her fawn crossed the path, just a short distance away from them.

"That's a good girl." John praised her for keeping a respectful silence, thus preventing the mother and her fawn from startling and running away.

He watched as both mother and baby daintily walked across the pathway and walked into the stand of trees that were just a short distance from the stony path. The doe had paused momentarily, to look in their direction, but must not have felt threatened by their presence. He always relished these opportunities to see some of nature's creatures at their finest. He preferred seeing them in a natural environment, as opposed to behind bars, in a zoological setting.

After they had disappeared into the trees, he and Lucy continued their walk. They had only gone a short distance when what looked like a baby squirrel came out from under some of the brush beside the path. Lucy suddenly stopped short to look at the strange little animal on the pathway before her. Then, to John's amazement, instead of darting back into the brush, the little creature began tentatively walking towards them.

"Shhh, Lucy," he softly whispered, "Let's not scare this baby."

Lucy sat completely silent and watched as the baby approached her. To John's amazement, the squirrel came close enough to look her in the eyes, and as quickly as it had appeared, it disappeared back into the bushes. Lucy yipped softly, as if to say goodbye.

"Well, that was a curious little critter, don't you think, little girl?"

Lucy yipped affirmatively again and began to tug on her leash, letting him know that she wanted to finish their walk around the lake.

As he settled Lucy onto the seat of his Escalade and buckled his seatbelt, he rotated his left shoulder forward and rubbed it once again.

"Ah, girl, I think I'm going to be glad to see the doctor later this month. I'm tired of the ache in my left arm."

Lucy tipped her head from side to side, as if that would help to process what had just been said. John loved it when she turned her head in that way.

"Sometimes, Lucy, I feel like you listen to every word. And I know that you understand a lot more than you're letting on!"

Lucy yipped, before lying down on the seat, in order to catch a quick nap during the ride home.

As John turned onto Lake Street, he slowed to look at his home as he pulled into the driveway. He had often thought of possibly selling the house. It was such a beautiful place and the grounds were impeccably kept by a wonderful man who came in for a few hours each day, to tend to all of the plants and trees on the property. Julie's handiwork was written all over everything. She was the one who had chosen which plants went where back when they had first moved in. Her decisions for the types of plants and colors looked as if they had been chosen by a professional. The flagstone pathways that wound their way around helped to enhance all of the landscaping that had been done and as everything had matured over the years, it had truly become their little sanctuary.

He smiled as he thought back to the day when someone who had been driving slowly past their property, stopped to ask John who had done their landscape design. John had chuckled as he'd told the man, "It was my wife's design. She did it on a large piece of drawing paper, using nothing more than a box of crayolas."

Though the house was much too large for one man and an eight pound dog, he had eventually made the decision to keep his life as it had been, while Julie had been there to share in it. He had faithful Carmen who came in on Mondays and Fridays, to cook and clean for him. He was relishing the thought of eating one of the meals that she had prepared for him to eat this evening. She was as good a cook and housekeeper as anyone could have ever had. She had come to work for them almost twenty years ago and she was like part of the family. Even Carmen, though, was getting older and he sometimes wondered how much longer she would be willing to stay.

As the garage door opened, he continued to sit in the drive, marveling that everything was still growing so well. The trees had dropped most of their leaves in preparation for the winter snows that would be coming any day, now. Many of the flowers still looked amazing, especially the pansies, as they seemed to thrive in the cooler weather. He could never understand how they managed to survive the winter. Their multi-colored beds could be buried with snow, yet when the warmer winter days came and melted off the snow, there they were, still flowering. As he gazed upon everything one final time, as he pulled into his three car garage, he sighed. Life had been very good to him. He had worked hard and God had blessed his efforts. As he considered everything, he again, felt reassured at the changes that he had decided to make to his will, while in David's office earlier that day. He had a sense of peace that his decisions had been the right ones. He was so happy with everything that he and David had agreed upon and he knew that Travis would one day, take care of everything as he had directed in the documents that he'd entrusted to his care.

Chapter Five

As Jamie sat at her desk, head down, she didn't notice her good friend, Sharon, come into the classroom.

"Jamie, are you all right?" Sharon asked with trepidation.

Jamie looked into the eyes of the woman she had taught beside for more than fifteen years, the person who had been there when Jamie had returned to full-time teaching after Matt's death. Sharon, with her robust figure and her ever changing hair highlights, seemed to be what attracted students and other faculty alike. She was the one whose ample arms were always ready to provide a hug to her co-workers anytime she noticed sadness in their demeanors. Sharon had taken time daily, to be there for Jamie, as she had haltingly attempted to get back onto her feet. Sharon was the one whose presence had enabled Jamie to get to the end of the school year, despite the numbness caused by the extreme grief of losing Matt.

"I'm okay, Sharon." Jamie replied.

"You don't look okay. Is it because the holidays are coming? And you'll have to face them without Matt beside you, once again?"

"That's the majority of it; after spending every Christmas with him since we met in college, this will be the second Christmas without him. I don't even remember last Christmas, but his absence from the holiday is starting to feel so permanent. And then,…there's this," Jamie said, as she reached into her desk drawer to retrieve a registered letter. "I signed for it last Friday. It was delivered right after the kids and I got home from school."

As she handed the letter to the one friend she knew that she could trust with the information inside, Sharon took the envelope from Jamie's hand and pulled out the documents that were nestled within. It took only a few minutes for the impact of the words to register in Sharon's mind.

"Are you kidding me?" Sharon angrily asked, "What heartless individuals would send this to a widow and her children when we're so close to the holidays? My gosh…I can't believe it!"

"First of all, Sharon, they don't know that I'm a widow. And although I feel the same way that you do, it's hardly the financial institution's fault that Matt died from such a rare cancer that the only treatment was determined to be experimental. When our insurance company denied coverage, I knew the chance that I was taking when I signed the papers for the second mortgage so I could cover the costs of Matt's treatments. I didn't even tell Matt what I was doing. He wouldn't have let me. But it was the only thing that might have helped to give him a fighting chance. At the time, I was willing to do *anything* to keep him here. I didn't want my kids to grow up without their father…and I definitely didn't want to be a widow. Not at this age. Actually, I don't think it would have been okay at any age. But life has to go on, in spite of difficult decisions that didn't work out in the way that we had planned." Jamie spoke, the defeat easily heard in the tone of her voice.

"What are you going to do?" Sharon asked, wiping a tear from her eyes.

"First, I'm going to have to tell the kids that the only home they have ever known is being foreclosed on, and that I plan to be moved out less than a month from now."

Jamie held up a hand to signal stop, when she saw Sharon begin to open her mouth to protest.

"Before you say anything else, I want you to know that this was the risk I took. I knew that my salary wasn't going to cover both the mortgage and the second, and I had to stop making payments some time ago. I'm just so thankful that Matt's life insurance covered what it did of the medical bills and all of the other unexpected expenses…which were exorbitant!" Jamie stated, "And I know what you were going to say…that I should fight this."

"Well, actually, yes, you know me well. What about Matt's parents? From what I remember, they have never lacked for money. There's no reason that they couldn't help to keep you and the kids in your home." Sharon replied.

"Matt's relationship with them had always been a little bit strained. I can't, no…I *won't* turn to the people who've never managed to take much time to invest in our lives or the lives of their grandchildren. I'd feel like I was betraying Matt. They've barely even been in touch with me over that past year. They continue to stay extremely busy traveling around the world with their friends. I don't want to be in a position where I'd feel like I owed them. That's just not me. It's times like this when I really wish that I hadn't been without my own parents for so very many years."

"I'm so sorry, Jamie. I thank the Lord daily, that mine are still around. Don't you think that Matt would want you to do whatever you could to stay in the home where you two had spent so many happy years together?" Sharon asked before adding, "Won't you at least think about talking to them, Jamie?"

"Oh Sharon, it's more than that. It's been so hard staying in the house without him. Not only has it been emotionally hard, but there are repairs that have had to be made, and snow to shovel, grass to mow…the list goes on. The kids have been great, but I don't want Ty to have to feel like he needs to be the man of the house. He's just a little boy. I want my kids to be able to be children, not 'homeowners'." Jamie spoke with resolve, "I think a little condo would be a good move for us. Then we can let a landlord take care of all of the things that are a challenge to me."

"But where will you go? Do you have any ideas?"

"Actually, yes I do. There are those condos on Bryant Street, just a few miles from here. They'll have a vacancy ready to go for me on December 1st." Jamie replied.

Sharon's brow furrowed as she considered what Jamie had just said. "The ones on Bryant? It's a bit of a rough neighborhood and those things are *really* small."

"I'm aware that it's not in the best part of town, but neither is this school. " Jamie said with a smile, "And if I just stick it out for a few years, I can hopefully save up enough to buy a small home again…eventually."

"It sounds to me like you've probably already made up your mind on this one." Sharon said, "Whatever you decide, I'm here for you. I'll support you in any decision that you make. I'll even stoop to the task of helping you pack!"

"I know, Sharon, that's why I showed you the letter of foreclosure. Not the part about helping us pack, although I figured pretty much that that's what you'd want to do. You have been an anchor for me ever since we started teaching together. I trust you like no one else and I can never thank you enough for being there when I needed you most. You *are* the definition of what a true friend really is."

Sharon wiped a tear from her eye before replying, "It goes both ways, Jamie. You were there to help me pick up the pieces when Dan walked out on me. And your kids are my like my own children! They're probably the only ones I'll ever vicariously have!"

"Speaking of your vicarious children, your vicarious son has a game today. Would you be interested in attending with Ali and me? Maybe they will even get a vicarious win that will keep them in the play offs!"

"Definitely interested, what time? Will I have enough time to go home and change into his school colors and get my pom poms?"

"Thankfully, yes. It's going to be an evening game, so Ali and I will plan on swinging by for you up after I pick her up from volunteering at the rescue, around 5:45."

"That sounds great; it'll give me a little time to grade some papers before we go."

"We'll text you when we're on our way. And Sharon, thank you for always being there for the kids and me."

"Aw, tain't nothin.'" Sharon replied.

Jamie had just risen from the chair behind her desk and given her friend a hug when the bell rang, reminding them that another day of teaching had begun. Sharon paused at the door, and then blew her friend a kiss, as she hurried out the door and headed to her classroom.

Chapter Six

"Hey Alison, I'm so glad that you're here! I've got four dogs that I need to take to have their teeth cleaned, and Jessica's running late. Will you be okay alone here for a few minutes?" asked Susan, the owner of Misfit Rescue Dogs.

"Definitely, with all these dogs around to protect me, I have nothing to fear." Ali answered with a smile, as she bent down to pet Susan's dog, Bailey.

"Okay, if you're sure then, I'll head out and get these pups to Dr. Smith's for their check-ups and dental work. I think most of them are looking at multiple extractions, so we'll be in need of more of the home made soft food. Will you ask Jessica to get that started when she comes in?" Susan asked as she grabbed her purse and keys.

"Sure thing, Susan." the teen replied.

"I don't know what I'd do without you and Jessica, Ali. And I don't know what these rescues would do if they didn't have you two around, either. You're life savers! I'll see you after I'm done dropping the new ones off." Susan said, closing the door on her way out.

"And, I don't know what I'd have done without these rescues." Ali said to herself as she and Bailey walked to the kitchen to get out the bowls in preparation for the Rescues feeding frenzy.

Ali pulled her long, blonde hair back and quickly braided it to keep it out of her face, pulling the hair tie from her wrist and wrapping it around the end of her braid. Securing her hair in a braid or a messy bun made it much easier when she bent over the different bins that held a variety of dog foods. Large kibble, small kibble, foods for older dogs, and younger dogs, and then there were the softer foods for the toothless dogs. The fridge held the home-made food that was fed the first few days after extractions. Ali was thankful that she had a list to follow whenever she was left in charge of feeding the furry pups on her own.

As she got out the list of dogs that were currently being kept at Susan's rescue, she felt a sense of sadness when she noticed that little Olivia was no longer among the names on the list. She saw the smiley face that was next to her name, along with Saturday's adoption date. Despite feeling glad that the little three legged pug must have finally found a family, Olivia had been around for a few months, waiting for a home. Most people wanted younger dogs and not everyone was into adopting the special needs dogs that had occasionally made their way to the safety of the Misfit Rescue.

Susan, the owner, had been a dog lover for all of her life and had a heart big enough to love every dog that she had taken into her home. She had seen how many pets were constantly being surrendered. Families tended to bring young pets home, but when they realized how much time and attention that ownership required, many of them weren't willing to invest all the effort that was needed. Surrendering pets to shelters was at near epidemic proportions. Some of the local shelters kept the pets for a period of time, but inevitably, for many of 'man's best friends', termination became the only answer.

Susan had focused on rescuing dogs, primarily from kill shelters. The kill shelters were most interested in adoptable dogs. Adoptable was interpreted differently by many shelters, but those shelters kept only the dogs that were the most likely to find homes. If a dog came in that was sick, maimed, or elderly, they weren't often seen as being adoptable. It was some of the 'unadoptable' dogs that Susan was also willing to rescue. She had built relationships with the local shelters in the city where she resided and many notified her as soon as they received dogs that weren't likely to find homes within the short time span that the shelter required.

A number of the dogs that Susan had rescued, like Olivia, had been simply been neglected or were elderly. Susan had realized early on, that she couldn't take all high needs canines or she would be overrun with too many dogs, just as so many of the shelters already were. There were many dogs that were overlooked, simply because they were so dirty and matted that they didn't draw the attention of families who were looking for a new pet. Some of them were young and all they needed was a good grooming and a little love, as they waited for a new home.

As Ali read through the list, she paid close attention to the dietary notes that had been written down. Three of the dogs were still on soft food while they waited for their mouths to finish healing from their tooth extractions. Fester and Bailey were on grain-free food, the smaller dogs were all on smaller kibble, while the larger dogs were on the higher calorie, large kibble. Ali set out ten bowls; each one with the name of a dog taped to the side of it, and began to measure the variety of dog foods into each dish. This was the easiest part of her volunteer job. Making sure that all the dogs went into their respective feeding areas to safely eat was often the most challenging. While poop scooping wasn't her favorite part of her volunteer responsibilities, she knew how necessary clean living areas were for her furry friends.

Walking and playing with the dogs was the best part of her job, hands down. Despite having to say so many goodbyes to the dogs as they came into and out of their temporary rescue home, Ali loved working there. The rescues always seemed to sense when Ali was most in need of love and comfort. Even the newest additions made sure to show affection if they noticed Alison's tears and sighs. The dogs were so fortunate to have been rescued, but in their own way, they had been the ones who had been rescuing Ali, ever since she had lost her dad.

Chapter Seven

"Hi sweetie, how did things go today?" Jamie asked, as Alison opened the door, hopped into the car and buckled her seatbelt.

"It was great, Mom. I aced the geometry test so it really made my day. I had studied hard and done all the homework, but I've never liked geometry as much as I do Algebra."

"That's wonderful! You and your brother really make me proud."

"And actually, it was thanks to Ty's help that I feel like I did so well. He seems to really have a knack when it comes to some of those angles, triangles, and all that stuff! Thank goodness!"

"How was he able to help you? He hasn't had geometry." Jamie replied as she looked at Alison, while wearing a puzzled look on her face.

"A couple of weeks ago, he sat down, read through some of the stuff in the book, took a look online at some of the things that I can access for additional information…and the little squirt, somehow, figured it out!"

Jamie laughed. "I don't think you should ever use that term when speaking to him. He's already sensitive to the fact that he's not as tall as you."

"Oh boy, you'd better believe it. I wouldn't ever call him a squirt to his face. He'd probably never be willing to help me with algebra again, and that would be a disaster for me! Although it wouldn't be quite as bad, now, as it would have been before he helped me. He's really good at explaining things in a way that makes sense. As a result, it's all beginning to sink in. You know what, Mom?"

"What?" Jamie asked as she merged into traffic.

"I think that we have the makings of another teacher, in the family. Ty would make a really good one, I think."

"Really?" Jamie asked.

"The way he teaches geometry makes me think that he'd make a good math teacher one day. He must get his gift of teaching from you. Some of your students have told me how much you've been able to help them get a better grasp on English. Yep, he'd be a good teacher, just like his mom."

Jamie blushed, as she relished such high praise from her daughter. "Wow, how do you suppose I ever got such an amazing daughter…and son, also?"

"I dunno, you just lucked out, I guess." Ali said with a smile as she began unwrapping the granola bar that she had found lurking in the bottom of her book bag.

"Since Sharon's place is just a few blocks away, would you mind texting her to let her know that we'll be there in about two minutes?"

"Shore thang, Mom." Ali said as she pulled her phone from the front pocket of her jeans.

"Sharon, sit down, please." Jamie laughingly requested of her friend. "The refs know what they're doing!"

Sharon sat and plunked her pom poms onto her lap as she turned to look at Jamie. "That was not an incomplete pass! Ty caught it and both of his feet were in bounds! I clearly saw it! And I can't believe that, as his mom, you aren't up in a tither like me!"

"Sharon, we're way up here in the bleachers. The refs are right there, down on the field, so they have a much better view of everyone's feet than any of the spectators do. I'm sure that the ref saw what he needed to make the call that he did…and, now, here they go again." Jamie said as she jumped to her feet, together with Sharon, and started to yell encouragement to the defense on Ty's team.

Alison looked at both women as if they each sported a third eye in the middle of their foreheads and shook her head, not quite sure that she was thrilled to be sitting right next to the two loudest women in the bleachers.

*Football…I don't really get it. They get four downs to make a down? Could they at least refer to them as something different, like call it four chances to make a down, or four downs to make a play…*As she looked up from her phone, she suddenly developed an interest when Ty's team held the line, the ball was kicked, and Devon Brown came back onto the field to resume his position as quarterback.

Ali quickly tucked her phone back into the pocket of her jeans, then jumped to her feet beside her mother and Sharon, and began to yell equally as loudly as the two women that she was standing beside.

As a very sweaty Ty loaded his duffel bag into the back of the SUV, Sharon was stomping up and down on her pom poms in the parking lot where they had parked and was muttering under her breath while she took out her frustrations on the two innocent inanimate objects.

"You were robbed! That was clearly a good catch that you ran all the way down to the end zone! I'm so mad at that referee's decision!" She said as she looked over at Ty, who was watching her trample her poor pom poms underfoot with an amused smile on his face.

"I know that it looked like a catch, and it was a great to catch that ball. But my left foot did go out of bounds before I had complete control of the football, so the ref made the right call."

"Well, I think that some of the rules in this game are just nuts…nuts, I tell you!" Sharon said as she picked up her mangled pom poms.

"It's okay, Sharon." Ty said as he came over to her and put one hand on her shoulder. "We were all really excited with how well we all played today. And we only lost by six points! The last time we played this team, they slaughtered us. At least we feel like we can hold our heads high this time, even though we lost."

"But, you're out of the play offs now." Sharon said with a pout on her face.

"It's okay, Sharon. The team hasn't even made it into the play offs before this year, so everyone's pumped. We're all determined to come back next year and fight even harder for the ultimate win!" Ty's optimism was obvious on his face.

As Jamie came to stand beside her son, the pride on her face was easily evident as she wrapped her arm around his shoulders. "You played great, Ty. I can't believe how good you've gotten at receiving."

"And you make a pretty darn good tackle, too." Sharon added. "Some of those guys are a lot bigger than you."

"Yah, but since I'm small, I can move really fast and they don't always see me coming, which puts me at an advantage."

"It's getting late, so we'd better head home since we all have school tomorrow. But where's your sister? Have either of you seen Ali?"

"I think she's over there," Sharon said, furtively pointing at someone across the parking lot from them, "talking to that boy."

"That's just Devon." Ty added.

"I think he's a little more than 'just Devon' to Ali." Sharon said as she winked at Jamie. "Are we now at that point in our lives?"

"What point?" Jamie asked.

"You know. The 'boy awareness point' in every girl's life. That time in our lives when we go from thinking that all boys have cooties, to deciding that they're not as creepy as we originally thought they were? After all, its happened to all of us."

"Oh, yuck." Ty interjected as he got into the car and added, "Can we go now? I'm starving!"

"Sure thing, honey. Just as soon as we can tear your sister away from your team's quarterback!"

Chapter Eight

Lucy danced around her master's feet, happily yipping and running circles around him, as he slipped his arms into his coat. John smiled as he thought to himself how Lucy couldn't be fooled. He felt pretty sure that she was an expert at understanding the time of day and she never missed a beat when he chose his clothing and footwear. As she had watched him slipping into casual clothing she had given one of her happy little whines. As they had headed down the stairs towards the entry closet, Lucy had taken the steps at a speed that amazed him. He would have tumbled down the stairs if he even tried to move half that fast. But then again, Lucy did have the advantage of four legs, not two. When he opened the closet door, she was right there, intently watching as he chose his running shoes. As he sat to slip them onto his feet, Lucy hopped and yipped with joy, as he began to tie his shoes.

"Yes, little girl! Since our nice weather is holding strong, we're going for a walk while we still can! With Thanksgiving just a couple of weeks away, we're bound to get some snow very soon." John said to the little dog that looked intently into his eyes and yipped, as if she had understood every word he had just said.

Once again, he paused to rub his left shoulder. This morning, however, it wasn't just the shoulder that was bothering him; it was his entire left arm that had begun to ache during the night. As much as he didn't want to possibly face another surgery, he was beginning to accept the fact that it might be something he would have to deal with sooner, as opposed to later.

Lucy stood onto her hind feet and happily approached her master and tapped him on his knee, as if to hurry the process along.

"Yes, little girl, I'm almost done and yes, we will be heading out in just a minute! Just be patient, I need a moment to catch my breath!" He leaned forward to pick his little black dog up and settle her onto his lap. Lucy turned around to face him and after putting both of her front paws on his chest, she proceeded to cover his face with kisses.

"Goodness, Lucy, that's an awful lot of kisses! Okay, girl, that's good now. My face is thoroughly cleaned and we need to get your leash on before we head out the door!" He never would have believed that he'd ever allow a dog, *any* dog, to cover his face with saliva! Somehow, though, as the years had passed, Lucy had managed to sneak in a kiss or two, and at times like today, she was allowed to show her love for her master by covering his chin with her kisses.

John took another deep breath before setting his rambunctious little dog back onto the floor. He rubbed his shoulder and arm once more, then stood to retrieve Lucy's leash from its hook inside the closet door.

He had just opened the closet door when it struck. Pain like he had never known before shot down his arm and back up the left side of his neck and jaw. The next sensation he felt was a crushing feeling in his chest. He continued to have the presence of mind to know that this wasn't just a shoulder issue. He felt sure that he was suffering a heart attack, as he reached for the phone on the entryway table right next to the closet door.

He plugged in the familiar number and heard the dispatcher say, "9-1-1. What's your emergency?" as he fell to the floor.

"Hello…hello…can you hear me?" the woman's' voice frantically asked. As she looked at the information on the electronic board, she was glad that the call was from a home phone. It provided the information that she would need to dispatch an ambulance to the address that was listed.

"Hello, hello, please, if you can hear me, please respond!" In the midst of frantic barking, she finally heard a barely audible voice say, "Chest…pain…help…"

And then the voice was silent. The only sound the woman continued to hear was the frantic yipping of a little dog in the background as the experienced dispatcher began to quickly co-ordinate the ambulance and EMT's, hoping to play a role in saving another life.

As her master lay silently on the floor, Lucy nudged him, much as she did in the morning when she wanted him to awaken. She hopped up onto his chest and began, again, to smother his face with her wet kisses. Normally, he would have reached up and stroked her. But there was no movement as he lay in silence.

Lucy stepped off his chest and onto the floor to begin running frantic circles around her beloved master. She continued to excitedly bark and nudge him, hoping to get him to sit up and continue with their planned morning walk. Lucy was determined to try to get him to respond, but no matter how loudly she barked or how hard she pressed her nose against his side, she was unable to arouse him. Eventually, she let out a sigh and a pathetic whine before settling down beside the only human that she loved with all of her little canine heart. She despondently laid her head on his chest and closed her eyes. The only move that Lucy finally made was to perk her ears, as she listened to the distant sound of a rapidly approaching siren.

As the paramedics approached the heavy front door, they hoped that they were going to find it unlocked. A door like the ones on the homes in this neighborhood wouldn't be easily broken into. As they ran up the steps of the massive home, they heard the excited barking of a dog. Thankfully, the latch had been unlocked, allowing them to open the door and enter with the necessary medical equipment that was capable of saving lives.

A wild blur of black fur rushed past them, only to turn around and rush back inside, to the gentleman who lay motionless on the floor in the foyer. The little dog began to jump on each of the men as they attempted to attend to her master's needs. She was quickly pushed aside over and over, as they checked for a pulse, put an oxygen mask in place, and prepared to use the paddles of the automated defibrillator, hoping to restore a pulse. The little dog's presence was problematic for the paramedics. Using the paddles would likely end the dog's life if she was anywhere near the body when they administered the shock to the heart.

"Hey Jake, can you grab this dog and hold onto her so that we can work?" one of the men asked of the newest member of their team.

When Jake bent down to grab Lucy, she easily eluded him and ran at the paramedic who was attending to John's lifeless body. Lucy jumped onto him, pushing her paws against him as hard as she could. If she had been a large dog, instead of the eight pound ball of fur that she was, she would have been capable of knocking him over. He quickly reached out and grabbed her by the scruff of her neck and handed her off to his co-worker.

As Jake held the little dog securely in his arms, she began to screech, emitting sounds that he had never heard come from a dog. His heart went out to the little animal as she frantically looked on, while they worked to resuscitate the lifeless body. While he softly petted Lucy, she finally began to cease her squealing and instead, she began to whine and in her own way, to cry. Jake had a deep love for dogs, so he found himself grieving for the little dog in his arms as he watched all that was unfolding before him. This was his third training run, but this was different from the others. They had included responses to a seizure, a fall from a tree, and a skater's broken arm. This was the first time that he had ever seen the medics work on someone who was in cardiac arrest. Despite being a traumatic situation, he knew that this was something that he had trained for and would eventually have to face. As he continued to hold the little dog, she began to quiver and he wished there was some way that he could help her to understand what was going on.

The medics continued c.p.r. as they loaded John onto the stretcher and began to wheel it to the waiting van. As Lucy watched from the arms of a stranger, she began her screeching once again and fought against Jake's grip as hard as she could, hoping to escape so she could get into the van. Jake held her tighter, to prevent her from hurting herself by jumping out of his arms, onto the ground. The last thing he needed was to see the little dog break her leg. He wished that he could take her along to the hospital, but he knew that his job was to deal with her as quickly as possible and get into the ambulance with the others. As he pulled the front door closed, he set her down and gave her a backward shove to prevent her from escaping and running away. Jake's heart was heavy as he listened to the heartbreaking howl of the little dog that he had left behind the closed door.

When Lucy's front paws began to feel raw from scratching at the door that had been closed in her face, she eventually let out a sigh and lay down, dropping her head between her front paws. She began to softly whimper as tears made their way down her furry face. She lay there momentarily, before getting up and walking to the open closet door. After stepping inside, she stood on her hind legs and reached for her master's neck scarf, hanging from a hook inside the door. After pawing it to the floor, she pulled it out and wadded it up in front of the door. She circled it a few times before lying back down and putting her head onto the treasure that bore her master's scent. As Lucy resumed her soft crying, she eventually drifted off to sleep.

Chapter Nine

"Hey, Em, did Travis call you?" John Jr. asked, as he shifted his cell phone so he could hold it in place with his shoulder.

"Yes, I just got off the phone with him and I'm on my computer now, looking for a flight in."

"Yah, me too. I found one that leaves a few hours from now. I went ahead and booked it. I should arrive by early evening."

"I'll let you know what I find and when I arrive. I think I can get there by tonight, also. Travis said that Dad's in intensive care, but things aren't looking very good. Did he give you any more information than that?" Emily inquired of her older brother.

"No, it sounded like it was a heart attack but the paramedics were able to resuscitate him in the ambulance on the way to the hospital. That's all I know, though." John Jr. replied.

"That's all the information that I got, too. I guess David, Travis and Mary are all at the hospital and will update us with any further information as it becomes available. I should probably hang up and get this flight booked. I'll see you at the hospital, then? I'm planning on taking a taxi from the airport to the hospital as soon as I arrive."

"I'll be renting a car when I get to the airport so I can drive us around while we're there."

"That works for me. I'll see you later, then," said Emily as she ended the conversation and turned back to her computer to finish booking her flight.

"I really hate hospitals." Emily said as they walked from the parking lot towards the large brick building before them.

"I feel the same', John Jr. said as he walked beside her. "In my mind, they aren't much different than a prison. If your health is bad and it's where you end up staying, it's almost as if you're held captive by the doctors and nurses who can refuse to allow you to leave. And if your health doesn't improve, you can be stuck there, against your will."

The large glass doors automatically slid open, as they came up the walk to the main entrance into the building, allowing them to walk into the seemingly sterile environment. Seated at the reception desk before them was an elderly woman, wearing one of the tan cloth over-shirts with the 'Volunteer' badge sewn onto the front pocket.

"How may I help you?" she asked, as they approached the desk.

"We're here to see our father; he's in the cardiac intensive care unit." Emily informed the woman.

"If you'll give me his name, I can look it up for you, in the computer."

"We already have all his room information." John Jr. said. "We'd just like some instructions on the best way to find the unit.

"Cardiac ICU is on the 6th floor. If you look to your right, you can see signs pointing you towards the elevators. Once you arrive on that floor, take a left and you'll see the reception desk where you'll need to sign in. They'll buzz you in through the doors to the ICU and one of the nurses will be able to help you navigate to his room."

"Thank you." Emily replied as she and her brother headed down the hallway to the elevators.

John Jr. and Emily sat quietly after being ushered into one of the hospital conference rooms, located a short distance down the hall inside the Intensive Care Unit.

"Why do all hospitals have the same smell that they had, back when we were kids having to get our tonsils taken out?"

"Hmmm?" John replied, finally looking up from his cell phone, to ponder what he'd just been asked.

"The smell? Like when we had our tonsils out?"

"I don't know, but you're right, they all seem to smell the same. It's probably all the cleaning products that they use. They probably get all of them from the same supplier, so it's always the same odors. Probably from a place called 'smell like a hospital.com'." he replied with a smile.

"Do you remember when we had to get our tonsils out?" Emily asked, since she finally had her brother's attention.

"How would I ever forget? I felt like it was so unfair that I was in there getting mine out at the same time as you! I wasn't the one who was always sick with tonsillitis. I wonder why they did both of us at the same time…maybe it was because they had a buy one, get one free campaign going on." John said, while elbowing his sister in the ribs.

"You might think that I was the only one who was sick, but I just had tonsillitis. You were the one who came down with strept throat every year, right after we went back to school."

"Yah, I guess you're right. I think that we were equally to blame for that unpleasant memory. At least we got to have all of the popsicles and ice cream that our hearts desired after it was all over and they finally sent us home."

As Emily dug in her purse for her cell phone, there was a light knock, before the door was gently pushed open, and David and Travis both entered the room. After exchanging greetings, they all sat down.

"John's doctor will be in shortly." David soberly informed them.

"How are you two doing?" Travis turned to ask. "I'm sure yesterday's phone call was a real shock."

"I think we're okay," John replied for both of them, "Dad was getting up there in age, so I guess it's never something that's totally unexpected."

"I think that's how it gets to be, as our parents' age. We know that their time here isn't going to last forever, but it can still be quite a shock when we receive the phone call, letting us know that something major has happened." David said, before continuing, "I have to admit that I was really caught off guard. I had just recently seen him and he seemed to be doing great. He and his little dog were walking daily, so I just never expected to get this call."

"Emily and I are both so thankful that you and Travis were the ones he'd listed as being the first to call in case of an emergency. How did the hospital know to contact you?"

"Your dad had information in his wallet and he had also had the information attached to the refrigerator door. It's another one of the places that the paramedics will check whenever they transport an unconscious patient. I'm pretty sure they got what they needed from either his wallet or from what was on the fridge door. As a result of the phone call, Travis and I were able to get here shortly after the ambulance arrived, so we were able to be with him since all of this happened."

After hearing a soft knock at the door of the conference room, Travis said "Come in." When the door finally opened, it wasn't the doctor, but one of the chaplains on staff at the hospital who entered first, followed by a cardiologist and another of the ICU physicians.

After cordially introducing themselves to John Jr. and Emily, the doctors nodded at Travis and David, acknowledging them again, after having spent time earlier in the day when they had briefed them on John's status. They had recommended that Travis and David get in touch with John's children as quickly as possible, and had suggested that they let them know the urgency of a timely arrival.

After the physicians took their chairs, the chaplain introduced himself to all of them. The look on his face belied his friendly introduction, as he, too, sat down.

The cardiologist spoke first, "John and Emily, let me begin by saying that we are so sorry to have to tell you that, though the paramedics were able to revive your father, it's only the machines that sustained his breathing," he paused, allowing everyone to process what had just been said, "when the paramedics had arrived at your father's home, they were unable to find a pulse, so they began CPR. They had no idea how long he had been without cardiac function when they began to work on him. It was during transport, after giving him a shot of epinephrine into his heart, that they were finally able to get a pulse."

"So, our dad is still alive?" Emily softly asked.

"His heart continued to beat on its own, but after arriving, the tests had revealed that his heart was only functioning at about twenty percent of capacity. He'd had a serious heart attack and the doctors here did everything that they could, to try to give him a fighting chance." The doctor explained. "I'm so sorry to have to tell you that in spite of every effort on his behalf, your father did not make it."

Both John Jr. and Emily sat quietly, as they digested what had just been said.

It was then that the chaplain spoke up. "We're so sorry to have to give you this news, and I'll be here for you if you need any help in dealing with your grief."

John and Emily looked over to Travis and David, the looks on their faces conveying the question that they had. "Did you know?" John asked.

"Yes, we did, however we wanted this news to come from the doctor, and not from us." Travis said, as he looked over at the siblings.

"Both of us and also, Mary, were with him the entire time, so I want to assure you that your dad was never alone, since arriving at the hospital." David informed them.

"And, again, I want to reassure you that everything that could have possibly been done for your father, was." The doctor spoke to reassure, "If your father had survived, we have no idea how long he had been without a pulse, but it appeared that it had been long enough that his pupils were unresponsive when he was assessed in the emergency department. In his case, it appeared that he had suffered major brain trauma, due to a prolonged lack of oxygen. In my opinion, as his doctor, it's probably for the best. He wouldn't have had much of a quality of life for any of his remaining time here."

"Please, no need to explain any further," John Jr. replied. "This is truly for the best. Our dad was always an active person, so I agree; this has turned out for the best."

As Emily began to dig through her purse again, the chaplain had noticed the moisture in her eyes, and gently handed her a box of tissues that had been sitting on the table next to him.

Emily wiped at the tears that had begun to slowly trickle down her cheeks. Softly, she said, "I guess that I feel about the same way that my brother does and we're grateful to all of you for tending to our father, especially in our absence…excuse me, please, I'll be right back." she said as she rose from her seat and quickly left the room.

"If you have any questions at all, about the handling of your father's care, please feel free to ask myself or my colleague." the cardiologist said, motioning toward the other physician in the room. "He was also involved in your father's care, so either of us should be able to address any of your questions or concerns."

"And again, if there's anything at all that I can do for you or your sister, please don't hesitate to ask," the chaplain said as he rose from the chair where he had been silently observing all that had taken place.

"Thank you, Chaplain, and thank you, Doctors, for all of your kindness in this situation. I feel sure that my father has been in good hands." John Jr. said as Emily quietly made her way back into the room.

As they walked out of the hospital, Emily turned to her brother to ask, "Since Travis gave us Dad's keys to the house, are you planning on staying there tonight?"

"No, I've already booked a room at the Broadmann Inn. What about you? Do you want me to take you there so you can also get a room?" John Jr. asked.

"I'm going to have you drop me at Sue's place, if that's okay. I thought that you and I could go over to the house in the morning, so we can begin making plans for what we're going to do with everything." Emily replied.

"Do you think that making plans so soon might be a little premature? Especially since Travis hasn't even scheduled the reading of the will yet?"

"I didn't say that we're going to do anything. I thought that we might just take a look around, to begin planning. I don't want to keep that monstrosity of a house, do you?" Emily inquired of her brother.

"No, I don't have any interest, either. I'd rather sell all the furnishings and the house and take the money. I enjoy my life just the way it is. I have no desire to move back here, nor do I want the responsibility of a house when I really enjoy having no maintenance responsibilities at my current residence."

"Good, then we're in agreement on that. I wonder how soon the will is going to be read." Emily wondered out loud.

"Travis said about two weeks from now, probably the week after Thanksgiving," John replied, "I think I'll head home as soon as the service is over and then I'll return for the reading of the will."

"I truly am so thankful that Travis and David are handling all the arrangements for Dad's service. I would have had no idea where to even begin."

"Yah, I am too. It sounds like Dad had pretty much laid everything out, so it's not going to be much of a burden for them, either. You know how Dad was, always thinking ahead and planning. All of his ducks in a row was how he always looked at things, so I guess it wouldn't be any different when it came to the end of his life…so, have you thought about what you'll do with your half of the inheritance?" John asked, curiously.

"No, I haven't gotten that far. I can still hardly believe that Dad is gone, it doesn't seem real yet. Maybe his service will help everything to begin to sink in. Plus, I'm sure that he left quite a chunk of change to some of the different charities that he and Mom always supported. As a result, we have no idea how much inheritance we're even going to be dealing with, so it makes planning anything a little difficult at this stage in the game, don't you think?" Emily asked, looking over at her brother as he pulled to a stop in front of her friend's house.

"You're probably right. I guess we'll know for sure in a couple of weeks." John said as he pushed the button to pop the trunk open.

As Emily reached for the handle to her door, she turned to John and asked, "Has any of this sunk in for you?"

"What do you mean?"

"I mean the fact that neither one of our parents is here any longer and we probably should have made a little more time for them, over the years?"

John thoughtfully rubbed his chin before replying, "I guess that I'm not exactly sure how to answer you and it's too late to ponder all of that right now. Whatever decisions I've made when it comes to time spent with our parents, I'll just have to live with."

"I guess the same goes for me. Good night, brother." Emily replied, as John pulled the car to a stop in front of Sue's house.

"Night, Em." He said as he reached over to give her a gentle hug, "Say hello to Sue from me. I'll see her when I come to get you in the morning. Is ten o'clock okay?"

"That works. See you tomorrow." Emily said as she grabbed her overnight Hermes bag from the back seat, exited the car and shut the door.

Chapter Ten

Lucy had slept fitfully through the night. John's scarf, between her front paws, had acted as a comforting pillow. Her paws were raw from rising to scratch at the front door throughout the night, but to no avail. She was still captive within the home that had once been a place of comfort that she had shared with her master.

As early morning approached, she had finally gone into the kitchen for a drink of water. After sating her thirst, she saw that there were still some nuggets of kibble in her dish, picked one up with her mouth and carried it back to the entryway where she laid it on the floor next to the pilfered scarf. After staring at the single nugget, she decided to let it lie and finally went up the stairs to the room where she had always slumbered on the bed at her master's feet, every night while he slept. After sniffing around the bed, she had rooted around, displacing the pillows and moving the blanket that lay at the bottom of the bed until it had finally fallen onto the floor. She had lain momentarily on John's pillow, savoring his scent. Her deep sigh signaled the sadness and the confusion that she felt, wondering where her master had gone and why he hadn't returned home. Lucy had lain down and had shed actual tears before hopping down onto the floor and heading back downstairs to, once again, wait by the front door.

Lucy perked up her head and listened closely to the voices that seemed to be coming up the front walk. She excitedly hopped up and walked to the door, staring up at the door knob, sure that she was finally going to run into the arms of her beloved master. She let out a soft whine as she tried to patiently wait for the footsteps to come across the front porch and listened as the key was slid into the lock. She rose up onto her back legs raising her front paws high into the air, expecting to jump into the arms of her master, once again.

As Lucy lay quietly in the back seat of the car, she continued to keep her paws on her master's scarf. In her little canine mind, she wondered where they were taking her and continued to hope that it would be to the place where she would be reunited with her master. She cradled her head on the scarf that had been wrapped around her when she had been lifted up into the unfamiliar car.

"Em…"

"Yes?"

"Do you think we're doing the right thing, taking Dad's dog to the shelter?" John Jr. thoughtfully asked his sister.

"I certainly don't want his dog. I know that she meant a lot to him, sometimes I felt like she meant more to him than we did!" Emily replied in a huff. "There's no way that I want to take on a dog, nor would I have time for one even if I did."

"I wasn't asking if you wanted to keep her, I'm just wondering if we should maybe try to find a home for her, instead of surrendering her to the pound." John replied.

"If you want to take the dog and try to find her a home, that's your prerogative. I just know that I won't have time to do anything like that."

"Yah, no, I wouldn't even know where to begin to look for someone to take her. Other than Travis, I'm not familiar with anyone who might be interested in taking Dad's dog and I'll need to fly home as soon as possible. And I doubt that Travis has the time to deal with the dog. He's probably already got enough on his plate, just preparing everything for the service." John hastily replied. "I've got some things to take care of in the next two weeks, before returning for the reading of the will."

"All right, it's settled then," replied Emily as she looked into the backseat at Lucy, "We take her to the pound and let them figure out what to do with her."

When the car finally slowed to a stop, Lucy raised her head and stood up onto her hind paws, allowing her to look out the window. She began to pant in excited anticipation of what might come next. As the back door was opened, Lucy was quickly pulled out the door to the ground, by the leash that had been clipped onto her collar ever since leaving her beloved home. Lucy let out a soft cry, as she jumped back into the car to protectively place her paws on the familiar scarf that had once belonged to her master.

"Good grief, come here you stubborn little thing!" Emily sternly stated, again pulling on the leash that was attached to Lucy.

"I think she wants Dad's scarf." John Jr. said, as he watched his sister pull the little dog from the car once again.

"That's fine with me if we leave it with her. Dad has no use for it now and there are some bloody paw prints on it anyway. I was going to toss it, so I guess we can just as well let his dog have it." Emily replied.

As John Jr. grabbed the scarf from the backseat of the car, Lucy excitedly began to follow him, never taking her eyes off her treasure. When the automatic doors opened she paused briefly to listen, as they all walked into a strange building that was filled with the cries and barking of so many abandoned animals.

Chapter Eleven

The young man at the desk couldn't help but notice the couple who came through the door with their reluctant little black dog in tow. They looked a lot alike, so he figured they must not be husband and wife, instead, they must be related; possibly a brother and sister, since they appeared to be similar in age. He stood several inches taller than she did and both of them had full heads of lightly high-lighted brown hair, so similar in color that it helped to confirm even more, the fact that they must be from the same family.

He was dressed in a well-fitted navy blue pinstripe suit, with matching vest and a bright blue necktie. His perfectly polished shoes looked like they had probably seldom been worn. The woman was dressed just as smartly as the gentleman. She, too, wore a tailored black jacket and fitted skirt. Her bright red blouse matched the heels that she was wearing, though, how she was able to walk in something like what she had on her feet, caused the young man at the desk to slightly shake his head in wonder. She also held a neck scarf in her hand, eventually dropping it onto the floor in front of the little dog, who immediately pounced onto it.

"May I help you?" He asked, coming out from behind the desk with his hand extended toward the gentleman.

"Yes, I hope so." The man paused briefly, reading the name tag on the young man's shirt. "Daniel, we'd like to see if you're able to take our dog, here. Family circumstances have suddenly changed and we won't be able to keep her."

As Daniel looked down at the little dog sitting quietly at their feet, he said, "Sir, this isn't a no-kill shelter. She looks like a sweet little dog and also, an expensive one; are you sure you want to leave her here?"

"Yes, we're sure." The woman holding onto the leash firmly answered.

"There won't unlimited time for her to find a home..."

"We realize that." The gentleman replied.

"There are some no-kill shelters; one is just a few miles down the road from here..."

"We have already discussed everything," the woman replied, "And we don't have a lot of time to run all over. We just want to turn her over to you so that we can be on our way."

"I understand." Daniel respectfully replied, even though he really didn't. "I'll need you to fill out the appropriate paperwork and then I'll take possession."

As soon as the paperwork had been completed and passed across the desk, the couple handed the leashed dog over and turned to leave.

"This looks like a really nice collar and leash..."

"Yes, it is, they're both high quality leather but the stones in the collar are just rhinestones, I'm sure. We won't need them or the scarf that she seems to have attached herself to; you can keep them for whoever might take the dog home." The woman said as the couple walked towards the door to exit the shelter as quickly as they had come, leaving the very confused little black dog behind.

When Susan hung up the telephone, she turned toward Ali and asked, "Do you have much in the line of homework to get done tonight?"

"Nope, I got everything finished up during my free period at school...why?" Alison asked.

"That was Daniel calling from the pound. He said that he's got a couple of pups that were just surrendered in the last couple of days. He thought that they might be a good fit here. I was wondering if you'd be interested in riding along with me when I go to take a look."

"Boy would I ever!" Ali replied. "Let me grab my phone and give my mom a call to ask her if it's ok."

"That sounds great, Ali. I'll finish up with the feeding frenzy and will see if Jessica can stay a little longer, while you get permission. Let your mom know that I'll drop you off after we're done." Susan said with a smile, as she returned to measuring out kibble from all the different bins of food.

As they were driving to the shelter, Ali began to prepare herself for the task that was ahead. The shelter that they were headed for was one of the ones where Susan got most of her rescues. In so many ways, she loved getting this opportunity, because it meant that she got to play a role in selecting dogs who were going to be well taken care of, until they found a new 'forever home'. In other ways, it was extremely difficult, knowing that so many others weren't going to get that same opportunity.

Each time that Alison had accompanied Susan on one of the rescue runs, she had learned to focus on the new rescues, offering loving comfort on the drive home, rather than all of the ones who had been left behind. Ali had always felt like she could never do what Susan did, she feared that she would want to rescue every animal that needed to find a new home. Susan had shared some of those same feelings with Ali as they had worked side by side for the past year. Alison had a deep respect for Susan's decision to give unwanted dogs another chance to find happiness and she was grateful for the opportunity to help with something that she felt was so important.

Ali let out a long repressed sigh as they pulled into the parking lot. Susan turned to look at her, knowing the mixed feelings that Ali was having, and asked, "Are you okay, Ali?"

"Sorry, Susan, yah, I'm okay. I just need to keep my eyes fixed on the new rescues and try to ignore the cries of the other broken hearted animals." Ali replied.

"I wish people wouldn't surrender so many animals, but at least we get to make a difference for a small number of those that have been abandoned." Susan said, as she put the van in park.

"Amen!" Ali answered, as they exited the van to walk into the building.

"Hey, Susan and Ali!" said Daniel as he looked up from the task he was working on at the front desk, "I think I have a couple of perfect pups for you. Let me pull the records that we have on them so you can take a look, before going back to meet them."

"Perfect, thank you," said Susan as she and Ali walked into the office that was situated to the left of the desk.

Daniel quickly retrieved the files that he was looking for and laid them out on the desk in front of them. "These are both older dogs," he said, opening a file and pointing to the information of a dog by the name of 'Rascal'. "He's 12 years old, eleven pounds and unfortunately, he's totally deaf. He's a sweet little guy, but he has been silently sitting with his nose in the back corner of his kennel ever since he watched his owner walk out two days ago."

As Susan perused the information, she read the brief information that had been written down when he had been surrendered. 'Family got a new puppy, and decided to surrender their older dog', she read. She knew that Ali must have read the same note, as she heard her softly sniff. A twelve year old, deaf dog would be in need of a special home. Susan found herself wondering if she should even consider him, knowing that it would take a while to place him. Despite feeling a little unsure, she wanted to see him, knowing that he would be high on the list of animals who might never find a home. She always took the time to look at any of the dogs that Daniel recommended. He seemed to always choose the best ones for her, the ones whose slim hope lie in the Misfit Rescue.

"I'm sure glad that my parents didn't get rid of me, when Tyler came along," Ali said softly.

"Isn't that the truth?" Susan replied to Alison's perceptive rumination, as she looked over at Daniel, who was completely distracted by another file.

"And this one is named Lucy." He finally said, opening the other file that was lying on the desk. "She's all black, ten years old and about six to seven pounds. She's such a little cutie, but you know how hard it is for black dogs to find homes, so there's a possibility that she might not make it out of here in time."

As he pointed at the information on the page, he added, "I was here when she was surrendered. It was a thirty-something couple who brought her in. All they said was that 'family circumstances had suddenly changed' when they handed her over, together with a man's winter neck scarf. She's very protective of her scarf, shrieks whenever she thinks anyone is going to take it from her. I think she came from a good home; she's been recently groomed and is chipped, so the information has been purged. I don't get it; she looks like a great little dog, other than a high pitched yip that can almost break your eardrums!"

"Well then, let's go and take a look," Susan said, as she and Ali rose from their chairs, to accompany Daniel down the hallway leading to the kennels that were located in the back of the building.

As Susan drove the van back home, Ali sat in the back seat with the two newest additions to the Misfit Rescue. Rascal lay on the seat next to her, head down and turned away, as if he was trying to avoid making any eye contact. He had looked so sad as he had sat in the back corner of the kennel, with his back to them. Rascal had made no sound and when Susan had reached into his kennel to gently turn him around, he had kept his head down. Both Susan and Ali noticed the tear stains on his face and when Susan had reached to pet his fuzzy little head, he had cowered, as if he thought she was going to hit him. Ali felt sure that that was the deciding factor for the eleven pound, matted mess of blonde fur. She knew that Susan had a special place in her heart for dogs that she suspected had been treated roughly. Susan always worked extra hard to find them a home where discipline would be given sparingly and gently.

Alison looked down at the little black fur ball that had immediately jumped onto the scarf in her lap, as soon as they had gotten into the van. Lucy, too, had stolen both of their hearts as soon as they saw her. She had lain, shaking, on top of 'her' scarf. As soon as Susan had opened the kennel door, Lucy had picked the scarf up in her teeth and begun to whine. When Susan took the little dog and her scarf out of the kennel, Lucy had frantically looked around, as if she was desperately seeking for someone. Ali's heart broke for the little dog, because she felt sure that Lucy sought the loved ones who were no longer a part of her life. Alison knew that feeling. There were times when she'd look into a crowd of faces, looking for her Dad, only to realize that he was forever gone from her life.

As Ali gently laid her hand on Lucy's back, the little dog looked silently up at her, her little brown eyes filled with moisture. When she carefully reached over to put her hand onto Rascal's back, he jerked only slightly, as if he knew that she had no intention of hurting him. Ali wanted to gather both of the little rescues into her arms and tell them that everything was going to be okay, but deep inside, she knew that they were going to have to go through a grieving process similar to her own. Loss was loss. At least in her case, she knew why her Dad was no longer around. These little dogs had to feel so confused, wondering what they had done wrong and the reason for their abandonment. Ali looked forward to giving some extra time and comfort to the newest members of the household. She also wished, as she had with some of the other rescues, that she could give them a forever home where she could be the one to love them back to wholeness.

Chapter Twelve

"Oh my gosh, Mom! School was great and this afternoon at the rescue was even better!"

"Why, what all happened, to make this a great day?"

"Okay, first, at school, I got an 'A' on another of my tests. I really didn't know if I could pull it off, you know that I'm not particularly in love with science, but I did it! And when I got to the rescue, Susan asked me to go with her to the shelter and pick up a couple of pups. I got to see Daniel again. He's one of the people who work there and he's just the nicest guy. And no, I don't have a crush on him. He's just fun to be around. He's always the one who lets Susan know when he has some dogs that he thinks would be a good fit for the Misfit Rescue."

"And?"

"And we brought two more dogs back to the rescue with us. They're both older dogs. There's a little black one, we think that she's a Moodle, named Lucy."

"And can you explain to me what, exactly, is a Moodle?" Jamie asked as she glanced over at her daughter, while navigating their vehicle through rush hour traffic.

"It's a mixed breed."

"Ah, so one is a poodle? And where does the 'M' come in?"

"The M stands for Maltese. So, she's a Maltese poodle mix, and she's so adorable! Some people call them Malti-poos. I usually just call them Moodle's. The other one is also a mixed breed, possibly a rat terrier and maybe a Sheba Innu. His name's Rascal and whenever I look at him, he makes me think of 'Benjie'. But the poor little guy is totally deaf, so he's this quiet and gentle little blonde dog. He looks so broken hearted. I'm sure that with his deafness, he's got to be feeling really confused by his new surroundings."

"It sounds like they're already trying to capture your heart, Ali. And I know how much you want a dog, but we just can't commit to one right now."

"I know. But for the next few weeks, I'll get to love on these two little dogs and I also get to play a role in helping them to find a new home. And, Mom, I'm planning on teaching Rascal some sign language while he's with us."

"There's that old saying that you can't teach an old dog new tricks, so you'll have to be very patient with him if he doesn't seem to be getting it."

"Once a teacher, always a teacher, huh, Mom?" Ali asked with a giggle. "I'll be very patient with him, but I don't believe that saying. We have a lot of older dogs who have learned all kinds of things that we weren't sure that they would be able to even comprehend."

"I have no doubt that with you as his teacher, Rascal is going to be able to learn all kinds of sign language."

"Thanks, Mom. I'll probably only have a couple of weeks, so I'm going to try and see what I can do while he's there."

"Oh goodness, we have to get over to the school so I can pick up Ty. The coach wanted all of them to stay after today, for his reaffirmation pep talk. He had some parent volunteers bringing in refreshments as his way of saying thanks to the team for a job well done."

"They really did play pretty well this year. I went to a few games last year, before Ty was on the team, and they *really* struggled. I think they only won one or two of their games."

"I wonder what the difference was, this year?" Jamie asked.

"I think it was Devon, Mom. He's a really good quarterback! His dad was transferred here from another state and when the coach had found out that he'd played quarter back for a few years, he made the decision to let him have his chance on the team this year."

"You seem to know quite a bit about this boy, Devon." Jamie said as she looked curiously over at her daughter.

"Yah, he's in a couple of my classes…and the rest was information that went around the school after football started. He's also been talking to me about my work with the rescues. I guess his dad was feeling guilty about moving him away from all of his friends, so he told him that he was considering getting him a dog."

"Does he want a puppy?" Jamie asked.

"Not since I started talking to him about adoption!" Ali smiled.

"Now why doesn't that surprise me?"

"I think that he and his dad are going to come by one of these days when I'm working. I think he's interested in a larger dog and we have some really great ones that are available right now. I told him that I'd be able to provide the information for any of the dogs that he might be interested in possibly adopting. Oops, Mom, I think that we might have just passed Ty! Oh, and look who's standing with him, it's Devon! If you pull over, I'll hop out and go back to get him for you." Ali said as she unbuckled her seatbelt and jumped out the door as soon as they had come to a stop.

"Now, why doesn't *that* surprise me?" Jamie spoke to the empty air, as her daughter hurried down the walk towards her brother and Devon.

As Jamie sat in the dark quiet of the living room, she still felt guilty that she had been forced to let Alison know that she wouldn't be able to bring either of the two new rescues home to live. Alison's request had been the impetus for sitting the kids down after they had gotten home, and telling them that they would be leaving the home that had once housed her precious family of four. The house where they had said their final good-byes to the Dad that they had felt would always be there for them. Both Ali and Ty had been really quiet as they had sat and tried to digest what Jamie had told them. They had just come from the 'high' of Ali getting a chance to spend a few minutes talking to Devon, who had been congratulating Ty for a job well done as one of his receivers.

Despite their silence, they showed that they could be good sports about the upcoming move, letting Jamie know that they understood why the move was going to be necessary. They had quietly accepted the fact that circumstances had dictated a decision that was impacting the security that they had all once known. Ali told them why she had done what she had, hoping to 'save their dad'. Both kids had agreed that she'd made the right decision. They were glad that Jamie had been willing to do whatever it took, that they might not have to face life without the father they had loved so completely. Shortly after the conversation had ended, both kids had headed up to their rooms. Jamie knew that they were trying to process yet another change in their young lives.

So, if she had really made the right decision, why had she felt so bad about telling her kids about the upcoming move? She sighed as she thought about how quickly life can change. She felt grateful that she was privileged to have the daughter and son that she did. Their resilience seemed to be one of their strongest traits. And for that, she was so very thankful.

Chapter Thirteen

"I feel a little frustrated that we only get Wednesday through Sunday off for Thanksgiving break this year." Jamie spoke as she stood at the door to Sharon's classroom. "If ever I had needed a full week off from teaching, this would be the year."

"I know! Right? I guess it's the district's way of making up for the additional time that we had off because of the plumbing issues that closed things down for a few days. I think that I've got most of my shopping done for Thursday, but if I find that I need anything else, I'll only have one day to shop for anything extra! I'm so glad that the four of us get to have our usual Thanksgiving celebration together again, this year. I felt so bad that I'd already booked tickets home, last year. If ever you needed me to be here, it was last year."

"After your Mom had been so sick, I wasn't going to hear of you cancelling your trip, Sharon. Besides, we weren't in much of a mood for celebrating the holiday anyway, and we were just fine without you."

"I'm not so sure how to take that last statement!" Sharon replied with a grin.

"You know what I mean. We weren't really 'just fine'. We made do in your absence. The kids were the ones who carried off the day, considering my own emotional absence on that day. So, I just need to ask. Is the turkey thawing yet? I hope." Jamie said, showing off her crossed fingers.

"Yes it is! It's busy hogging most of the room in my refrigerator while it takes its dear sweet time to defrost. I totally learned my lesson a few years ago when I took it out the day before.

Remember? I had to bake it with the giblets still inside and I didn't think that stupid bird was ever going to get done!"

"I still find myself laughing about that little faux pas." Jamie replied. "Although, I'm not one to talk! I still remember the first Thanksgiving dinner after Matt and I were married. Talk about a disaster! We had packed the dressing so tightly into the turkey that as it swelled, it split the bird in two. And when the dressing came out looking like a football, it was so tough and rubbery that we had to cut it into slices with a steak knife! What a hoot. Matt and I never got beyond bringing that disaster up every year when the holiday rolled around."

"Well, maybe this year, we can pull off a winner for the day. Do you think it's a possibility?"

"One can always hope, can't we?" Jamie said as she turned to go back to her classroom. "Let me know if you want me to bring anything else, okay?"

"Will do. But I think I have everything. Thanks, Jamie."

As Jamie heard the phone ringing, she wondered who would be calling this early on Thanksgiving morning.

"Oh my gosh, Jamie! I've got a problem and it's a major one!"

"What, Sharon? It's only 8:30 on Thanksgiving morning, what happened?"

"Well, remember that I had to get a new stove back in September?"

"Yes, how could I forget? We must have visited twenty stores before you were able to finally make up your mind. Is the stove not working?"

"Yes, Jamie, it's working. I was so proud of myself. I got up, made the dressing, gently stuffed the turkey, settled it into the pan…the lid even fit on nicely…and I put it in the oven."

"That sounds great, so, what's the problem?"

"When I went to set the oven to bake, I accidentally set it to clean! And it locked its door because it's all electronic and it's holding the turkey *hostage*! And I can't get the door open! Jamie, I'm *cleaning* my turkey! And the oven is getting so hot that it's going to be one big lump of coal if I can't figure out how to cancel the clean!"

After Jamie burst into hysterical laughing, she was finally able to collect herself enough to ask, "Can't you just hit the cancel button?"

"This isn't funny! I tried cancelling it, but it's not responding! And, why are you laughing? Again, this isn't funny!"

"I'm sorry, Sharon, but oh yes…yes it is! This would only happen to you!"

"Well," Sharon also began to laugh, "Maybe you're right. Why should this year turn out any differently from some of the other celebrations that we've had. And it wouldn't be so bad, but I can't remember where on earth I put the manual so that I can see how to make this doggone thing stop cleaning my bird!"

"You're in luck, Sharon, because I remember. After your stove was delivered, you said 'Jamie, don't let me forget that I put the manual in the cupboard above the fridge'."

"Oh my gosh, yes, now I remember too! You're a life saver! Gotta go!" she said as she hung up the phone.

While Jamie stood listening to the dial tone, she burst into laughter again as Ali and Ty walked into the kitchen, wondering what was going on.

"Oh goodness, kids, you're never going to believe what Sharon just did to the turkey!"

As Ty leaned back onto Sharon's sofa, he rubbed his stomach and asked, "When do we eat dessert?"

"Seriously, Ty?" Sharon asked. "You just told us how stuffed you were."

"I *am* stuffed, but didn't I ever tell you about my two stomachs? One is for food and the other one is for dessert?" He replied with a mischievous grin on his face.

"That's my brother for you. He came up with that story when he was about five years old and he's been telling us the same thing ever since."

"And that's my story, and I'm sticking to it, Sis."

"Well, it's still a few hours before the stores begin to open for their Black Friday sales, so we have some time to come up with our game plan for which ones to hit first." Sharon said as she looked over at the kids.

"And it's enough time for you two to help us finish cleaning everything up, too." Jamie said as she opened the dishwasher and began loading it with dishes.

As Ali and Ty carried dishes from the table, Ty asked, "So, if everyone is shopping on Thursday, why do so many people still refer to it as 'Black Friday?"

"Tradition." Came Ali's one word answer, "About like football, why do they get four downs for a first down?"

"Tradition." Was Ty's quick retort.

"Are you sure you don't want to go shopping with the kids and me?" Sharon asked as she finished rinsing and putting the dessert plates into the dishwasher.

"I'm positive. You know how much I dislike shopping in the first place. And I'd do anything to avoid doing it in the midst of days like today…which turns into a total shopping frenzy!"

"I think there's something really wrong with you, because I can't imagine a woman who doesn't like to shop! You must have a genetic defect, or something." Sharon looked skeptically at Jamie.

"You might be right, Sharon."

"Yah, Mom always told me that she thought she suffered from the female shopping gene deletion. I'm just glad that she didn't pass it on to me!" Alison added, while stowing the leftover pie in the refrigerator.

"Even I like to shop, more than Mom does and I'm a guy!" Ty interjected, while pushing the chairs back under the table and setting Tom the Turkey back in its place of honor, as the centerpiece. "So, how soon before we leave?"

"Just a few more minutes and we'll be ready to go." Sharon answered as she turned to Jamie. "I'll bring the kids home as soon as we're done. Do we have a curfew that we have to keep?"

"No curfew of any kind. Just bring 'em home when you get sick of them."

"Gee, thanks, Mom. Do you really think that Sharon will ever get sick of us? She might get sick of Ty, but, surely, never me!"

"Hey! Is that how you're supposed to treat the younger brother who looks up to you?"

"Yah, right, you look up to me only because I'm taller." Ali commented, as she looked at her brother with a smile.

"Hey, lay off! I might be shorter for right now, dear sister…but one day soon, I'll be towering over you!"

"Ty's right, Ali, it probably won't be long before you look up to him! And, don't forget to take some money for any shopping that you want to do."

"I'm not going along to shop; I'm just going as a spectator!" Ty replied to his mother's suggestion.

"I've got my money; I'm definitely not going as just a spectator!"

"I hope that all of you can have a little fun as you battle the crowds! Now, why don't the three of you skedaddle and I'll finish everything up here before I head home."

"Okay, then…on this note, it's time to hit the stores. Grab your coats, kids, and head out to my car. The weathermen said that we might even see a few flakes begin to fall tonight. And, Jamie, don't forget. Tomorrow evening is the Parade of Lights. We're all going to go again this year, aren't we?" Sharon asked.

"Absolutely! After all, it's been a tradition!" Jamie reminded her friend.

"Oh yay!" the siblings echoed one another in agreement as they slipped on their jackets and followed Sharon out the door, to her car.

Chapter Fourteen

As Jamie heard the ping of the microwave, she got up off the couch, skirting the boxes that were stacked in multiple places throughout the living room. As she walked into the kitchen, she moved the boxes that had been set next to the microwave, allowing her some space to mix peppermint hot chocolate into the cup of water that had been heating for the past minutes. She savored the aroma while the mixture dissolved in the cup as she stirred. Once thoroughly mixed, she made her way back to her spot on the couch, to resume staring into the fireplace at the flames being emitted by the gas log.

As the mesmerizing flames captured her attention, her thoughts had begun to drift over the activities of the last weeks. Ever since she had told the kids about their impending move, all three of them had started working together, sorting, disposing of items, and finally packing the things that were the most important to them. The three of them had gone together to look at the little condo that would soon become their home and despite being a fraction of the size that they were used to, they had all brainstormed their ideas on how to fit everything into the new surroundings when the time came. Sharon had kept her promise and had spent her spare time helping them to pack boxes as they prepared for the move.

As Jamie pulled both knees up under her chin, she rested her cup on one knee while warming her hands on the hot chocolate brew contained within her favorite snowman mug. After taking a few sips, she set the cup onto the coffee table in front of her and picked up her computer, hoping to resume the Christmas letter that she was intent on finishing before Thanksgiving weekend was over and classes resumed on Monday.

Knowing that she still had a few more hours before the kids returned, hopefully, she had decided to tackle her Christmas letter. As she looked down at the blinking cursor on the computer screen, she was reminded that the only thing she had written so far was the greeting, "Dear Family and Friends,"... There had been no letter last Christmas, so attempting to summarize the past year seemed to be a reasonable subject to attempt. The question was, how do you communicate to others in a manner that won't make them feel bad as they celebrate Christmas? Do you tell them that your idyllic twenty year marriage had been reduced to nothing more than a beloved memory? Definitely not uplifting, especially considering the time of year and the fact that Christmas Eve was exactly one month away.

As she hit the back button, she deleted her original greeting and replaced it with, 'Merry Christmas, from our home to yours,' pausing again and hoping that her writer's block would miraculously abate, to allow not just the start, but the completion of a task that Jamie deeply desired to check off her list of things to do.

After setting aside her computer and picking up her cup to take another sip of the rich hot chocolate, she finally had some clarity of mind and, after returning an empty cup to the coffee table, she set her computer back onto her lap and began to type.

Once again, she read her opening salutation, approving it in her mind, before resuming her writing. 'I thought it would be nice for all of you to know that we are managing to survive, ever since Matt left us. I also know that since I didn't write a Christmas letter last year, I didn't want to ignore this most blessed time of the year again, wanting rather, to wish everyone a Merry Christmas.

It's been more than a year since Matt left us for his eternal home in heaven. What can I say, other than 'life goes on'...somehow. His absence is felt daily by the kids and I and the house feels so very empty without his calm and gentle presence. We have, all three, missed sharing our lives with him. At times, the reality of his absence is still able to take my breath away. There were times in the early days, when I felt like my heart was so wounded that I couldn't comprehend how it was even able to continue beating. I am thankful that mine was able to continue to beat at all, after saying that final goodbye. I truly believe that if it wasn't for the love of my children, co-workers and friends, I could have easily died of a broken heart.'

Jamie sniffed and wiped a few tears from her cheeks before resuming.

'As I think back to last Christmas, I have a hard time believing that more than a year has already passed. As the fog of loss began to lift, I was reminded of so many special friends who have been there to support us, as their way of showing respect to a man who was beloved by all who ever had the privilege of getting to know him. The kids and I know that so many prayed for us as we embarked on the journey of grief that was forced upon all of us. Those prayers helped to sustain us when we felt like it would be impossible to move forward in a positive manner. And as this year has passed, we all seem to be doing okay. I want to thank all of you for all the support you gave us in a variety of ways. We couldn't have navigated any of this journey without you.

I continue to learn how to navigate life without my protector, provider and the love of my life. He was always the soothing balm whenever I felt like going ballistic, and believe me, there have been many irritations that have tried to drive me over the edge! One of the first things I had to deal with after losing Matt was a sprung sprocket on the garage door opener. (I didn't even know that garage doors had sprockets, let alone that they could spring! And I had no earthly idea where to even begin to look for a garage door sprocket!) And the doggone door is so heavy that it was no fun opening it the old fashioned way until it could be fixed. I also managed to run over a nail with my car on the same day that the sprocket sprung…yep…a nice little leak. Add to that, the front door knob that decided to stick itself shut (when the garage door was on the fritz, of course). I decided that I had seen enough T.V. shows that made kicking in a door look easy…NOT a good idea! All I did was hurt my foot, but at least it did cause something to go 'click' inside the knob and I was finally able to get the door open. Thankfully, the knob has continued to work ever since then.'

Jamie couldn't help but smile momentarily, as she thought back to some of the incidents that had been mandated by Murphy's Law when she had least needed them.

'I'm not sure I should even mention the beeping smoke alarm at 3 a.m. Of course, it couldn't be the one that I can reach on a small ladder…nooo…it had to be the one at the top of the peak in the great-room. I was sure that Matt wouldn't want me up on a 20 foot ladder while the kids peacefully slept soundly in their beds, so it beeped until the next day when a wonderful neighbor came over to rectify the situation when he got off work that afternoon. Lo and behold, a week later another one decided to start beeping at midnight, so the search for the pesky culprit was on, and it took hours before I finally found it! (I never cease to be amazed at the fact that kids seem to be able to sleep through anything!)

Adding to that, my SUV's engine light decided to come on for no apparent reason, especially since it had just passed its 36,000 mile check-up 500 miles earlier! Oy vey…all I can say is that it's good that I don't own a gun. If I did, we'd be looking at the stars through the holes in the roof where I would have blown the beeping alarms to kingdom come and I'm sure the front door and the car would both be sporting fatal wounds, also! So, at times, it has either been laugh or cry. I've cried a lot more than I've laughed, but as the year has passed, I'm realizing that things won't always be this way. I truly believe that one day, the smile and laughter will come from the inside once again.

Now, for some brief updates:

Alison and Tyler are both attending the same middle school this year. Ali and Ty have been great support for one another and I am glad that they are together at school, once again. They're such great kids and were there for me when I had no idea how to go on. They were my anchor, when unfortunately, I should have been theirs. They continue to have good grades and Ty continued to play football, in spite of the fact that his Dad was no longer giving him encouragement from the sidelines. Ali is a volunteer for a woman who rescues unwanted dogs until she can locate permanent homes for the poor, abandoned pups. Alison thoroughly enjoys showering love on the rescues. I think it has played a huge role in the healing that is slowly taking place in Ali's life. I continue to teach High School English and I accepted a full-time position when I returned to teaching last January, after a six week hiatus. I enjoy helping to foster a love of language and writing in my students and delight in being there as not only a teacher, but also, as a friend. Teaching has been some of the healing balm in my life.

Again, I want to say how much we appreciate all of you and to let you know that we *are* making some headway as we continue to carve out a new normal in all of our lives. Life is good, even when times are hard. I hope that you are able to find the time to celebrate the reason for the season. As I bring this letter to a close I wish all of you the best, hoping that as you celebrate, you rejoice in knowing that Jesus is the Reason for the Season. Have a Happy New Year,
Our Love, Jamie, Ali and Ty'

'P.S. If the return address on the envelope looks unfamiliar, it's because that will be our new address on December 1st. We've decided to relocate to a condo that is closer to the kid's school and also to the school where I teach. I figure that this way, I can allow our landlord to take care of the things that I lack the patience and skill to do on my own!'

After Jamie hit the save icon for a final time and closed the lid on her computer, she heard the raucous sound of laughter as her children and Sharon exuberantly tumbled through the front door.

Chapter Fifteen

"Look, Mom, there's an empty parking space!" Ty said, as he pointed to one lone spot that was left open in one of the lots near downtown.

"I'll jump out and save it!" Sharon said as she proceeded to open the door to Jamie's small SUV, jump out and run like a banshee for the empty space.

"I'm not sure that we're going to fit." Jamie said to Sharon as she rolled the window down, looking skeptically at the small space.

"You can do it, Mom." Ty reassured her, as he, too exited the car to take a better look.

"What's your opinion, Ali?"

"Go for it, Mom. We might have to think 'skinny' when we open the doors to get out, but this thing is small enough that I bet it's going to work. In fact, I'll get out now, so you can leave a little extra room on your side."

As Jamie inched her vehicle into the tight space, she wasn't sure how much she appreciated the three 'cheerleaders' who were encouraging her as she slowly pulled in between the two vehicles parked on either side of her own. When she had finally stopped and turned off the ignition, she carefully opened her door and walked sideways, to allow just enough room for her to exit the vehicle.

"When we come back, I think you guys will have to let me pull out so that you can get in without having to get squished."

"Sounds like a great plan to me, because I don't think I can 'skinny up' enough to squeeze in through the door." Sharon spoke with certainty, as they all broke into laughter. "I'm so glad that we always come early enough to get a pizza at Bambinos Pizza every year. I can't even imagine trying to find parking just before the parade begins!"

"I agree, but it's beginning to look like people are showing up earlier and earlier each year, hoping to get parking well before the parade starts." Jamie replied.

"Mom, will you pop the hatch so we can get the chairs out? I'll carry two of them, and Ty will grab the other two."

"I'll get the blankets, if you'll grab the thermos and the cups." Jamie said to Sharon as she and the kids began handing things out from the back of the vehicle, before beginning the three block trek towards the restaurant.

"What kind of pizza are we going to order? I'm starving!"

"When aren't you starving, Ty?" Sharon asked.

"Never!" Ty answered.

"We can vouch for that!" Ali and Jamie answered at the same time.

Every year, on the first Saturday after Thanksgiving, the community sponsored the Parade of Lights. The floats were just as the title indicated and were all lit up with colorful lights, helping to usher in the Christmas season. When the parade had originally begun, there had been few floats. The parade had consisted primarily of cars or trucks decorated with lights, carrying small groups of Christmas carolers and others dressed as seasonal characters. As time had progressed, the parade had become the highlight of the city's season, bringing hordes of people from miles around, to the city's downtown shopping district.

All of the shop owners had begun to take advantage of the number of shoppers that the parade brought in, each turning their respective stores into a virtual winter wonderland. The entire city had begun to embrace the seasonal tradition that ended with the lighting of the tree in the center of the park that was nestled in the center of the downtown shopping area.

The city itself had gotten onboard, also, in the decorating that was done each year. Gone were the old decorations that had hung precariously from the light poles that lined Main Street. Some of the older, inexpensive decorations had been packed and unpacked so many times, that it was sometimes difficult to tell what its original characteristics had been.

The city had raised the funds to purchase new decorations for sprucing up the main area in the city's heart. No longer did worn out, obsolete decorations flop around in the wind, but instead, remained solidly on their pole, adding to the festivities of the season. Not only were the decorations newer, but all of them were lighted, to include the large 'Merry Christmas' banner that hung across the street at First and Main.

The parade had progressively gotten to be more interesting, also. Many businesses had begun to promote themselves through the intricate floats that they had begun to sponsor. In the early days, there had only been one or two marching bands that had participated in the parade. Each year, the numbers of schools had increased, each putting their own spin on some of the most popular Christmas songs. They had also gotten to where most of the musicians had some kind of lights on their musical instruments or uniforms, making their presentations that much more enjoyable, as they marched and danced down the street.

When Alison and Ty had been small, their favorite part of the parade had been the different groups who had ridden horses, decked out in Christmas reds and greens, some even wearing blinking lights on the reins that helped to keep them in control. They had also really enjoyed the elves that had marched down the street, throwing candy at the many children who had lined Main Street.

The potentially biggest problem that was encountered each year during the Parade of Lights weekend was the inconsistency of the mountainous weather. Some years, the participants enjoyed above zero temperatures, making the two mile march really enjoyable, not only for them, but for all of the spectators, also. Other years, they marched in temperatures that were well below freezing, causing everyone to bundle up like Ralphie's younger brother, in "A Christmas Story". During the almost twenty five years that the parade had been in existence, they had only had to call it off twice, due to blizzard conditions that would have made travel nearly impossible.

This year's parade had been met with nearly perfect circumstances. The weather hovered near the freezing point and the forecasters had suggested that spectators might even find themselves being sprinkled with a light dusting of snow, before the parade's ending.

As the final float had gone past, being followed by the street sweepers, everyone lining the street had begun to gather their chairs and belongings to begin the walk towards Centennial Park.

"Wow that was such a great parade this year." Ty said as he shifted the bags holding the sling chairs onto his shoulder.

"It just keeps on getting better and better all the time." Ali added, "And next year, I'm going to be *in* the parade, instead of watching on the sidelines!"

"How so?" Sharon asked.

"Because next year, Susan want's to have a float for the Misfit Rescues in the parade, to help continue to raise awareness. All of the volunteers will have the option of riding on the float and we'll even be bringing some of the dogs who aren't too excitable, to ride along."

"Oh, nice, that sounds like it's going to be fun." Sharon replied. "Who's going to make the float for you guys?"

"Susan hasn't gotten that far, yet. But I think that a lot of additional volunteers are going to be needed to help us with putting a float together!"

"Maybe your mom and I can help to generate some interest among some of the students and teachers who might be interested in lending a hand."

"Susan is planning on putting information together, to try and generate interest. She said that she'll probably circulate flyers sometime late next summer or fall so that we have plenty of time to prepare."

"I don't know how she already does everything that she does for all of these little rescues." Jamie said as she dropped some trash in one of the receptacles that lined the street. "I don't know where she gets all of her energy. She still works full time, doesn't she, Ali?"

"She does. She's gotten to where she doesn't keep quite as many dogs in her own place; she's gotten a lot of new foster families who have recently come forward, so she cares for less dogs than she did in the past." Ali answered.

As they continued to make their way down the street, they noticed a number of families, especially those with smaller children, had begun to head for their cars.

"The tree lighting makes it kind of nice for those who stay behind." Jamie said as they continued on with the die-hard crowd that was heading for the park. "The number of people always thins out enough that the traffic isn't bad by the time we're ready to leave, thank goodness."

"And the fact that we always stop for a quick snack, in order to feed your son's voracious appetite, makes it even better." Sharon said as she gave Ty a little nudge. "So, where do you put all of that food anyway?"

"I think it's all going to his feet," Ali added, "haven't you noticed how large they've gotten to be? They look like a couple of boats attached to the bottom of his skinny legs!"

"Hey! That's no way for you to talk about your younger brother! I'd never talk about you that way!"

"Oh yah, right. Who was it who always made fun of me back when I had to wear 'train tracks' on my teeth?"

"I was just a kid back then. What did you expect?"

"Ty, that was only two years ago, you weren't that much of a kid and you were determined to make me feel self-conscious about those dumb braces!"

"Mom…Ali's being mean to me." Ty said with an exaggerated whine in his voice.

"Ali, be nice to your brother." Jamie said with a smile, as they approached the large pine tree that was growing in the center of the park. "Man, this tree is getting huge!"

"I know; I was looking at some photos of some of the earliest tree lighting ceremonies when I took my students to the historical center. It's a miracle that the poor thing didn't fall down from the weight of all those decorations in the early days! I mean, they really went nuts with the decorations. And the lights weren't these little tiny ones like they use today. They were huge bulbs!"

As the four jostled into place near the tree, they could hear the beautiful sounds of the symphony playing traditional Christmas carols from their places in the band shell. On the bleachers that had been set up near the tree, was a choir dressed in white robes that had been accented with alternating red and green stoles. The choir stood in place, keeping their eyes on their director, who was getting ready to have them begin to sing along with the symphony band.

As they began to sing the carol, 'Oh Christmas Tree', a light snow began to fall.

"Oh, wow," Jamie softly gasped, "this is truly beautiful. What an amazing way to wrap up a perfect evening."

When the choir and the band finished the song, they stopped to allow the mayor to step up to the podium for the lighting of the tree.

"Is everyone ready" he asked.

"Yes!" the audience collectively responded.

"Then, here we go with the countdown! Five," As everyone joined in, the counting became raucously louder, "four, three, two…one!"

The entire crowd, to include the choir, all broke into applause as the switch was thrown and the tree seemed to spring to life with lights, while animated Christmas decorations sprang into action from the electrical surge. As the snow fell gently onto the branches of the tree, it looked as if it was being supernaturally flocked by the hand of God himself.

As the snow continued to fall, the crowd was thinning out as everyone began to head back towards the vehicles that would take them to the warmth of their own homes. Except for Jamie, the kids and Sharon, as they all headed for the McD's that was just up the street from the park, in order to feed an always hungry teenage boy.

Chapter Sixteen

"Well then…that meeting went about as well as we had expected it to go." said Travis, as he looked over toward his father. "I'm thankful that you were here. Not a great way to end the week after Thanksgiving. Thank goodness that it's Friday and I have a clear schedule for the rest of the day! I think I'll just go home after lunch and chill in front of a movie for the afternoon. Preparing for this meeting with John and Emily has made for a really stressful week!"

As David looked up from the legal documents that he had been perusing, he looked into the eyes of the son who made him feel proud. Travis's professional demeanor had always been one of the characteristics that helped to make him into such a successful lawyer. As he carried on the family practice, John had no doubts that it would continue in the same way that it had originally been established. His law office had always come highly recommended by his clients and he'd found that word of mouth advertising had been the very best way for his business to grow in the way that it had.

"John had always hoped that I might still be around when this day came, especially after the changes he had decided to make a few weeks back." David replied. "I still can't believe that this has happened to him. I feel frustrated with myself. When we last saw one another, he was complaining about the pain in his shoulder…"

"Dad, you can't blame yourself for what happened to John." Travis said as he brushed some dust from the sleeve of his Italian suit jacket.

"I know that I shouldn't blame myself, I just wish I had thought that maybe his pain could be related to his heart and not just another shoulder problem. He might still be okay, if he had gone to see a doctor sooner." David's remorse was easily detected in his voice. "I guess I wasn't ready to say good-bye to a lifelong friendship like the one John and I shared. It was hard enough when Julie passed away and now, in a sense, he's gone, too. I just can't believe how quickly life can change…in an instant."

"You and Mom have always reminded me that life is fragile and life can change in the blink of an eye. Have no regrets, Dad. This isn't your fault."

"I know, and your mother and I have always reminded you that life isn't fair. And this seems very unfair."

"Dad, are you and Mom taking good care of yourselves? I know that you both eat healthy and exercise, but are you keeping regular appointments with your doctors?" Travis's concern was easily heard in the questions that he had asked.

"Yes, we are; and your Mom and I are planning to be around for a good, long time yet. Especially your Mom, she's continuing to hold out for those nebulous and future grandchildren!"

"I'm well aware of the fact that Mom is still hoping for grandchildren, especially while she still has her mind and before she gets too old to realize what a grandchild is!" Travis said with a wink and a smile.

"One of these days, Son…one of these days you'll meet the woman of your dreams, just like your old man did!"

"I already met that woman, Dad, but she changed her mind and I just haven't gotten around to having any desire to put my heart on the line again."

"We understand; no pressure from your mom and me. We just want you to be happy, but we also realize that happiness isn't found in another person and we recognize how much your career has helped to fulfill you."

"Yah, my career is really fulfilling…except when it comes to days like today!" Travis replied, "Did you see the shock on John and Emily's faces when they learned that each of them was only going to inherit a set amount of money and not the entire estate, to include the house?"

"I can honestly say that I probably would have reacted no differently if I had been in their shoes." David thoughtfully replied.

"No, Dad. You wouldn't have referred to that amount of inheritance as a 'pilfering amount of money' and made it sound like it was next to nothing. I know you. Both you and John worked hard to get to where you are. I have clients who would give *anything* to receive that amount of money, even if it was just once in their lifetime. For some of my clients, that money would go a long way to positively changing their lives forever."

"Trav, you have to admit that they were somewhat blind-sided by the will and the fact that they didn't end up being John's executors. Not only did they learn that a majority of the estate had already been committed to a number of charities and John's foundation, but then, to learn that Lucy was going to be the recipient of an inheritance, also…I bet they're wishing that they hadn't surrendered that little dog so quickly."

"Dad, that's the other problem that I'm having…I didn't even think about Lucy right after John died. He'd be so heartbroken if he knew his little dog had been taken to a shelter. I thought that Emily had said she was considering staying in the house, until we had the meeting regarding the will. I had just assumed that she would have kept Lucy with her, at least until after that had been taken care of. They had to know that their dad would have made some kind of arrangements for his little companion and that it would have been stipulated in his wishes. I was almost hoping that Emily would have formed an attachment to Lucy and decided to keep her. Dad, it's my fault that Lucy was taken to a shelter and I'm going to have to do everything that I can in order to track down that little dog."

"Sadly, Travis, it might have complicated things even more if Emily or John had decided to keep her. Would they have kept her just long enough to be able to take possession of the additional inheritance and then get rid of her? Would they both have decided to work things out together or would it have turned into a battle between siblings? Today, when they learned that the decisions had been made jointly while both of their parents had been alive, they probably realized that they can't even contest everything by declaring that John wasn't of sound mind. He and Julie were definitely of sound mind when they made the decisions about Lucy seven years earlier. The only other things that John had recently changed were the increased amounts for charity, and the reduction in the original amounts for John and Emily."

"No matter what, Dad, I just hope that I can somehow find that little dog. Just knowing how important she has been to John, I feel almost desperate to locate her. I just hope that John Jr. and Emily left her at the 'no kill shelter' that they said they did. If not, and she went to the other shelter, she would have had limited time to be adopted into another home."

"Can you imagine how your mother and I are feeling? *We* should have been the ones to make sure that Lucy was safe. She was supposed to come and live with us! I promised John that your Mom and I would take care of her, if anything ever happened to him. I was sure that we'd never be faced with giving Lucy a home. I was sure that she'd be gone long before anything ever happened to John. Your mom and I had discussed things and we were both fine with taking custody of Lucy and overseeing her inheritance. We had already decided which of John's favorite charities would benefit from what Lucy had received, because we had no need of any of her money."

"I'm just glad that John had come up with every contingency when it came to Lucy, except for the part where she was left at a shelter! Even though I wasn't fully in agreement with everything that he had decided when it came to Lucy, he knew that I would honor his wishes and carry out my role as he had trusted me to do so."

"Travis, everything always has a way of working out okay and I'm going to trust that this will too. Lucy might have found a home in time."

"Yes, and if she has, that will complicate things even further. How will I deal with wrestling her away from someone else who might have already fallen in love with her?"

"I think that Lucy's inheritance can be a helpful way to give someone a monetary bonus for taking care of a dog during this mix-up. Either way, if there's anything that I can do to help you find her, please, just let me know."

"Thanks, Dad. I appreciate the fact that you and mom have always been on my side…well, almost always." Travis looked towards his father, with a wink and a smile.

"Okay, Son, let's not even go there. Your mom has finally found it in her heart to forgive you for enlisting." David laughingly replied. "Actually, your Mom is so proud of your impressive character development *because* of your enlistment. John was equally impressed and that's why he had no reservations about turning the handling of his estate over to you. He trusted you to take care of everything in his absence and often wished that his own children had made some of the time for him over the years, like you always had. I'm sure that John Jr. and Emily are terribly disappointed with today's knowledge, but then again, maybe this will be the catalyst for them to move forward into a future that they have both put off for far too long. That's what John was hoping."

"The biggest problem in all of this is the fact that John *trusted* me with Lucy, too. I feel desperate to find that little dog. She's just got to be okay. I've got to find her as soon as possible."

"I have a lot of peace about all of this, Trav. As I said earlier, everything, I'm sure, will be okay. But for right now, after the 'excitement' of this day, I'm hungry. Since all of this unpleasantness is behind us, would you like to get some lunch with your old dad?"

"That sounds great, especially if my 'old Dad' is the one who's going to pick up the bill." Travis replied as he and his father rose from their seats and prepared to leave the office together.

Chapter Seventeen

"Finally! The last box is unpacked! And, it's only the first day of December! I am so very thankful that they were willing to let us start moving into this place a few days earlier than what we had originally planned." Jamie said as she looked around the small and very cramped living room. "What do you guys want to do to celebrate this special occasion?"

"Pizza and sodas!" Ty replied, letting his two hollow legs do the 'talking' on his behalf.

"And a movie and popcorn after pizza might be nice." said Ali with a smile.

"Pizza delivery, ok? And a movie, here, or at the theater?" Jamie asked.

"I'd prefer here, I'm really tired," Ali replied as she looked down at her shirt and jeans, soiled from the dust and dirt that had come off of the moving boxes, "and that way, I don't have to get into the shower, change my clothes, do my hair…you know how it is, Mom."

"And heaven forbid that she go out in public looking dusty like me! I wouldn't shower, I'm just fine the way I am!" Ty replied as he gave his sister a playful punch in the arm. "I'm not tired at all, but I'm okay with staying in."

"So do I get a say in any of this?" Sharon asked, "Because, I'm on board with Alison. A shower sounds great, but I'd prefer to do it after I get home and then I can get into my fuzzy jammies and call it a night."

"And Mom, don't forget, I have to be up early tomorrow. We're taking the rescues down to the pet store for the next three weekends. We want to give the dogs as much exposure as we can before people run out and buy new puppies to give as gifts. Susan is hoping to get some of the rescues placed into their forever homes in time for Christmas." Ali added.

"Okay then, pizza and a movie at home is what the general consensus has chosen. I have to admit, I'm totally exhausted." Jamie replied as she began to pull up information on her phone, "And thanks for the reminder about tomorrow, Ali."

As they sat around the small table in their new environment, no one had much to say as they munched on pepperoni pizza and salads. Ty was managing to eat two slices to everyone else's one.

"So, Ali, what will you be doing tomorrow…I mean, when you take dogs to the pet store?" Sharon looked at Ali and asked, as she continued to observe Ty's ability to wolf down his pizza in record time.

"We meet the other foster families and their dogs in the store parking lot, prior to the store opening, usually about half an hour before." Ali thoughtfully replied. "We usually set up three or four z-pens inside the store, near the back. After getting the dogs out of their kennels, we'll get them dressed before we group them together in the different pens."

"What? Did I hear you right when you said that you *get the dogs dressed*? Why do you dress them and what do they wear?"

Ali giggled and swallowed before answering, "Since it's getting close to Christmas, we'll dress them in seasonal gear. Some of them will just wear Christmas bandanas; others will be in little elf and Santa shirts, while the more skittish will probably just have a Christmas bow put on their collars. I'm so excited. I found the cutest little dress that I'm going to put Lucy in and Rascal's going to wear some striped doggie pajamas."

"When you put the dogs together in the pens, don't some of them fight when you put them together?" Sharon asked.

"That's a great question, but no, they all seem to get along okay. I think that so many of the dogs are so thankful to have been rescued, that they usually seem to be on their best behavior. And since most of them are with multiple other dogs in each of the foster homes, they're used to being around different dogs so they're pretty accepting of being temporarily penned with the other dogs that are brought to the store. We do try to keep some of the foster dogs together, because they feel more secure that way. But we always have a separate pen for the older dogs. We put a sign on the pen so people know that they're the senior dogs."

"Do the people who come into the store to shop just wander back and find you?" Sharon inquired.

"We always do some advertising on the web site and the stores advertise, too. A lot of people know that the first and third Saturdays of the month are when the rescues will be at the store, so we get a good turnout of people who are primarily there to take a look at the dogs that they've already seen on the web site. Many of them already have a dog in mind before they come in. This month, Susan has added one additional Saturday for 'Meet and Greet'." Ali explained.

"Ahhh, that's so cute. I've been to a meet and greet before, but it was to meet men." Sharon smiled. "Are the families allowed to take the dogs' home with them that same day?"

"No, they aren't." Ali replied. "They get to hold them and walk them, do a little cuddling and snuggling to see if it's going to be a good fit. If they decide on a dog, then they fill out the paperwork and Susan schedules a home visit within a day or two. After she's convinced that the dogs are going to good homes, the adoption becomes final…and another rescued dog finds a family to love, who will help to make them feel loved again, too."

"Wow!" Sharon's eyes got big. "It's a pretty involved process!"

"Yes, it is," Ali replied, "it's to make sure that the dogs go to good homes, forever homes. They've already been through having their little doggy hearts broken, so Susan and the other foster parents want to be sure that it won't happen again."

"I'm so thankful that Ali's a part of these rescue efforts." Jamie said proudly.

"I am, too!" Tyler added. "In fact, I'm hoping that one of these days, we can become a forever home for one of the pups she helps out," he said as he looked at his mother with pleading eyes.

"You know…one of these days, it's going to happen." Sharon said, as she winked at Ty and smiled at Jamie.

"O...kay...," Jamie turned toward Sharon and smiled. "I don't need you to encourage these two. Believe me; they need no help from anyone!"

"Oh, I'm not encouraging them. I'm just stating a fact!" Sharon said, gently clapping Jamie on the back as she rose from the table and headed for the kitchen, with her dirty dishes in hand.

As Jamie finally collapsed into bed, she was careful not to wake Alison, who was already softly snoring in the twin bed across the room. She was glad that they had finished the unpacking as quickly as they had, allowing them to eat a late afternoon pizza and finish the movie earlier in the evening, as opposed to later. She couldn't believe how exhausted she was, now that the packing and moving were finally over. She felt like she had been running on adrenalin alone, for the past few days. She was also feeling a sense of accomplishment, along with the relief of knowing that she was doing okay, despite feeling like she had just closed the door on another chapter of her life.

"Would you be proud of me, Matt?" she whispered to herself as she snuggled deeper into the warmth and coziness of the twin bed that had previously belonged to Ty. She hoped that he was enjoying a good night's sleep in the bed that had once been hers.

As she turned to look at Matt's framed picture on the nightstand beside her bed, she looked lovingly at the beloved and familiar photo. *We did it. The kids and I did it, Matt. We downsized and packed our entire home. And we managed to get it all done without you there beside us. You were always the one who was so great at organizing, sorting, and even stacking boxes. But, Matt, we did it. I'm so proud of our children; I wish you could be here to see what fine individuals they are turning out to be. You'd be so very thrilled. I can't help but wonder what you would think of this place? It's awfully 'cozy' and it makes me feel like we are now a part of the tiny home movement!* Jamie stretched her arms above her head as she yawned and smiled.

As she reached over to turn off the light, she first picked up Matt's photo and stared at it as a tear slipped silently down her cheek. She sighed before setting it down, then clicked off the lamp and rolled over, hoping that she might once again see her beloved husband in her dreams.

Chapter Eighteen

The doors on the back of Susan's van were open when Jamie and Alison pulled up in front of the house.

"I'll call you when we get back from the meet and greet, Mom. It probably won't be until around two, though, because I'll help Sharon unload the pups and I'll clean kennels after that."

"Sounds good, I'll wait for your call then." Jamie replied, as she watched Ali exit the car and walk over to bend down and pet one of the dogs that Susan had just brought out through the front door.

As soon as all of the foster's had arrived in the pet store's parking lot, each one began unloading their precious cargo in the parking lot. Ali and several of the extra volunteers had already carried the z-pens into the store and set them up in the back, near the dog food. After returning to the parking lot, everyone began working together, carrying crates and leading the larger dogs into the building through the automatic sliding doors.

Ali had grabbed the small kennels that were holding Lucy and Rascal, while Susan carried in two of the larger ones.

"Ali, if you'll stay inside the store with these four pups, I'll come back out to get the others. The dog clothes are in the black bag that you carried in with the pens. Make sure that Lucy and Rascal stay together. He's somewhat dependent on her for security, since he can't hear what's going on around him. The 'Seniors' sign is also in the black bag."

"Sounds good, Susan. You can count on me." Ali enthusiastically replied.

"I know I can, Ali. That's what helps to make my job easier. It's the fact that I *can* count on you!"

Alison blushed as she began to rifle through the black bag, looking for the costumes that she wanted for dressing Lucy and Rascal. Once she had wrestled Lucy into her Christmas dress, she began to tackle Rascal, who had decided that he had no desire to wear a striped red jumpsuit that looked like Christmas morning pajamas. As Ali petted and loved on him, he began to calm down enough that she was finally able to get him dressed. Once she had finished dressing both of them, she placed them into the pen for the senior dogs and began to put the scarves and bows on each of the other dogs from Susan's rescue, and corralling them inside their respective pens.

She smiled as the pens began to fill with other colorfully dressed canines. All of the dogs were wearing Christmas colors, so it began to feel very festive, especially after Ali and one of the other helpers finished stringing ribbon around the outside of the pens.

Just as they were finishing up, after filling water bowls to set inside each of the pens, they all heard "Ho, Ho, Ho!" coming from the front of the store. Since it was the first day of December, the pet store had scheduled Santa 'Paws' to come in on Saturday mornings, throughout the month of December. He would be here for the next four weekends, allowing people to bring their pets in for pictures with the jolly old man.

Ali smiled and waved at him as he came to the back of the store, where he set his large red chair near the rescue pens.

"Hello, Alison." He said as he situated the velvet chair.

"Hi Santa," she said with a smile, "it's nice to see you back again this year."

"This tends to be one of the highlights of the Christmas season for me. And these days, I'd much rather play Santa to a bunch of furry children. Even though some of the pups can get a little grumpy, at least they don't take one look at me and begin to scream for their mother! Some of those screams can be a little too 'ear piercing' for these old ears!"

"Little Lucy here, has her own 'ear piercing' abilities when she barks."

"Remind me to prepare myself if she decides to sit on my lap!" he broke into laughter as he took a seat on his velvet throne, as the store officially opened its doors for the day.

Ali felt a deep sense of sadness mixed with one of relief, as she noticed that neither Lucy nor Rascal were spending much time outside of the 'Senior' pen. There were two other older dogs in the pen together with them, who spent most of their time being ignored, also. Because Lucy looked so cute in her little dress, and because she was only eight pounds, she was at least being handled by a number of shoppers.

One older couple had latched onto her, planning on taking her home, until they learned that she was ten years old. Since they had just lost their own dog about six months earlier, they made the decision to leave Lucy behind and had selected one of the younger dogs instead.

Alison tried to be patient with people, thankful that they were planning on giving rescued dogs as Christmas gifts, instead of new puppies. But it still broke her heart that too often, the older dogs ended up being over looked. After more than a year of helping at the rescue, Alison realized the benefits of adopting the older dogs. They tended to be well potty trained, they never chewed up furniture or shoes and they were content to sleep and go for short walks. She had also seen how some of the older dogs tended to settle in a lot easier, seldom trying to run away to go and look for their previous owners.

Alison almost always spent most of her time near the older dogs. She took every opportunity to speak on behalf of the seniors and some of her encouraging talks had resulted in people being willing to open their homes and hearts to one of the older dogs. This Saturday, Alison found herself being quiet on the subject of elder dog adoptions. Somehow, she just couldn't bring herself to being the one to encourage the adoption of Lucy or Rascal. She realized how much she desired to make them a part of her own family.

As the morning had progressed, it ended up being a very successful meet and greet. Nine families had filled out the adoption paperwork. Even one of the older dogs had managed to find an older couple who wanted to commit to giving him a home. Alison was secretly elated that she would be loading both Lucy and Rascal into their carriers and taking them back to Susan's to stay for a while longer. As much as she wanted them to get forever homes, Ali wasn't ready to let go of the two little dogs that had captured her heart ever since she had helped to bring them home to Susan's.

When Jamie pulled into Susan's driveway, she saw Alison talking to, of all people, Devon. She couldn't help but notice how glowing her daughter's faced looked, not to mention the mesmerizing look that Devon wore, as he and Ali interacted. It took only a moment before Alison noticed that her mother was there to pick her up. She raised one of her hands and held up one finger, to signal 'in a minute' to her mom.

It was just about that time, when Jamie noticed a tall man come walking out of the rescue, talking with Susan, who walked beside him. Jamie immediately suspected that the man was more than likely Devon's father. The two looked too much alike, not to be related to one another. They stood at about the same height and had identical sandy colored hair. Their builds were similar and they were both dressed in jeans and polos, making the resemblance even stronger, though Devon's polo was red and his father's was a dark forest green.

As they approached Ali and Devon, Susan looked over and waved at Jamie. She also, held up one finger, just as Alison had done. Since everyone was smiling, Jamie began to surmise that another successful adoption was about to happen, especially when she saw the man take Susan's hand into his own, and shake it, as if to seal the deal. In a few short minutes, Alison and Devon had said goodbye and each of them had parted to go their own way.

As Alison jumped into the car, the smile on her face almost said everything that Jamie had wanted to ask her about. "So, I assume that you have good news?"

"Oh my gosh, Mom! What a day this has been! It's been the *best*!" Ali said as she buckled into the front seat.

"So, fill me in."

"Okay, well, first of all...Lucy and Rascal didn't get adopted today."

"Aw, I'm sorry to hear that."

"No, Mom, don't be. I wasn't ready to say good-bye to them, not just yet, anyway. Eventually..." Alison's voice trailed off momentarily, before she resumed her summary of the day's events. "One of the older dogs was able to find a home. An older couple wanted to adopt Max, he lives with one of Susan's foster families, he's an older pug, but he's all personality. The couple said that since they were older, they didn't want a long term relationship! Cute, huh? Anyway, they will be picking him up next week. They spent a fortune while they were in the store and that dog is going to get more Christmas presents than a lot of people get! And...this is the absolutely best part of the day!"

"And that part would be?" Jamie asked, while smiling at her very exuberant daughter.

"Well, I know you saw me talking to Devon...and that was his dad talking to Susan."

"I suspected that, because they both look so much alike."

"I know, right? I had been talking to him about the rescues and his dad decided that he could pick out a dog, to bring home with them before Christmas! When they came to Susan's, she hadn't even told me that they were coming, I was back cleaning up...well, you know. This afternoon Devon came back and found me because he wanted my recommendations for a dog! Mom, he's just the nicest person...anyway, he and his Dad followed me around while I introduced them to the larger dogs and I gave them all the background on each of them." Ali paused to take a sip of water from the bottle that she always kept in the pocket on her bag. "Anyway, they made the decision to adopt Parker. He's a golden lab; only about four years old and one of the friendliest dogs that you can imagine. He was exactly what Devon had in mind, when he began thinking about being able to get a dog. And his dad really liked Parker, too."

"So, it was a good day for some of the rescues, then."

"It was, Mom. Nine of the dogs that had been taken to the pet store found their forever homes! They're going to have families in time for Christmas! Mom, it was just the best day, ever!"

Jamie suspected that ending the day with Devon's visit to choose a rescue had been the 'icing on the cake'. As Alison's phone buzzed, she quickly pulled it from her pocket, and smiled.

"Anyone important?" Jamie asked.

"It's just a text from Devon. He wanted to say thank you for helping him to choose a dog. Do you think I should respond?"

"Definitely. Or at the very least, send him a smiley face emoji." Jamie smiled as she watched her daughter begin to type on her phone. *Just Devon? Yep, I think it's finally begun to happen. Boys no longer have cooties.*

Chapter Nineteen

As the doors of the shelter slid open, the volunteer looked up to see a tall man, smartly dressed in an expensive looking navy blue pinstripe suit, come through the glass doors and approach the desk.

"Sir, how can I help you today?" the elderly woman asked, as she laid down the pen that she had been using to work on the crossword puzzle in the newspaper that was open on the desk.

"Yes, I'm hoping that you can help me. My name is Travis, and I'm here to ask some questions about one of your dogs."

"That's wonderful, sir. We have quite a number of dogs who are more than ready for adoption. Do you have a specific idea in mind on the characteristics you'd like your dog to have?"

"I'm sorry," Travis hesitatingly replied, "I'm not here to adopt a dog. I'm looking for a dog that would have been surrendered a couple of weeks ago."

"Okay, I'm just here manning the desk today while the head of this shelter is out until tomorrow, so I'm not sure if I'll be able to answer any questions that you might have. I feel sure that Daniel will be able to help you once he returns."

"I just came from the no-kill shelter and they had no record of the little dog being turned over to them, although that's where I had been told that she had been taken. I'm hoping that if she was taken here, I'm not too late to find her."

"If she was surrendered here a couple of weeks ago, sir, then either she was adopted in a short time or, sadly…" the volunteer didn't bother to end the sentence.

"Would it be possible for me to at least go back and take a look at the dogs that are being kept here?"

"Yes, sir, most definitely. Let me get one of our volunteers to come to the desk and lead you back to see the dogs that we currently have in our facility." The woman said as she reached over to press the buzzer that would signal the volunteers who were working in the back.

It took only moments before a young man came out to the front desk to escort Travis down the hall to the noisy area where all the crying animals were being kept. As the woman watched Travis walk through the doors into the back, she hoped that his suit wouldn't attract too many of the loose hairs floating around the place.

She was deep in thought, attempting to come up with a nine letter word that would fill some of the final empty spaces of her crossword puzzle, when Travis returned through the door. She couldn't help but notice the way his shoulders drooped as he walked toward the desk.

"No such luck, sir?"

"No, I'm afraid that little Lucy wasn't back there. Here's my business card, ma'am. Would you please make sure that Daniel gets this when he returns tomorrow?" Travis sadly asked.

"Most definitely, sir. I'm so sorry that you didn't see your dog. I hope that she was taken home by a good family."

"This is such a sad place, whatever made you want to be a volunteer here?" Travis asked.

"I love animals. I'm at an age where I don't want another one of my own. If anything happened to me, it would be another broken hearted pet that would be left behind. So, I decided that I can at least come here and shower love on the animals that are brought into the shelter. I usually work in the back when Daniel is here to 'man' the desk. Even though it's emotionally hard, I can take the time to show love to the animals that are surrendered. Some of them will be living out their final days while here. Everyone who volunteers spends as much time as possible showering those animals with love. It's the final gift that we can give to them. For some of them, they receive a short period of tender, loving care and attention, hopefully knowing that in their final days, they were loved." The woman replied, as she wiped a small tear from the corner of her eye.

"Ma'am, I'm so sorry, but I'm also thankful that you're here for these animals. You deserve a medal for the work that you do. I can honestly say that I don't think I'd have the courage to do the same. I appreciate your willingness to share these things with me. I'm dearly hoping that the little dog I'm seeking was able to find herself a home."

"You know, we do keep very accurate records. I'm sure that when Daniel returns, he'll be able to help you learn what happened to your dog. In the meantime, I'm going to be praying that she was one of the dogs who were able to find a home."

"Thank you so much." Travis replied, as he turned to leave the building.

As he sat in his car, Travis was finally able to let some of his own tears make their way down his cheeks. He felt such a sense of sadness as he sat and remembered the sad cries of so many of the animals that were being held within the shelter. Many of them had looked so totally defeated as they hung their heads in sadness. Others had just lain there, making no sound, like they had no desire to find another family to love; they just wanted their old family back. Still others had jumped and barked, as if they thought that by getting someone's attention, they might receive a deeply desired reprieve from the kennels that held them captive.

As he put his BMW in reverse, intending to back out and head home, he saw the volunteer wave at him as she came running out of the shelter's front door. As he rolled his window down, she quickly walked over to his car.

"Sir," she started to say.

"Please call me Travis, ma'am. Sir makes me think of my father." He said with a smirk.

She couldn't help but notice the deep dimples in each of his cheeks when he smiled. "Travis it is, then. Please call me Josie."

"Is there something that you wanted to tell me, Josie?" Travis asked.

"Well, yes, I don't want to give you any false hope, but, did I remember you refer to your dog, as Lucy?"

"Yes, Lucy was her name. She was a small black dog, I think she might have been part poodle and part, hmmm, something else."

"Oh good, now I'm excited!" Josie replied. "One of the volunteers said that they thought they remembered a small black dog named Lucy being picked up by one of the dog rescues that's located here in town."

"Oh Josie, this is such good news! Do you have the name of which rescue organization that it might have been?"

"That, sir…I mean, Travis, I can't tell you. Our volunteer didn't remember, he just remembered that a little dog named Lucy and one other dog were both picked up and taken from the shelter together. I'll leave a note for Daniel with this additional information. I'm praying that you might be able to find your little dog!"

"Thank you so much, Josie. You just added some sparkle to an otherwise depressing day. I'll be anxiously awaiting Daniel's call. You have a wonderful day!"

"And you, too, Travis." Josie replied before heading back into the building.

Chapter Twenty

As Alison and Susan pulled into the driveway at Susan's rescue home, checking off another Saturday of finding new homes for the dogs, Ali punched auto dial on her cell phone to call her mother, who was waiting at home for her call.

"Hey Mom, can you come and pick me up in about half an hour?" Ali asked.

"Sure thing, honey. That will work out great, because I need to run Ty over to Andrew's house shortly. As soon as I finish dropping him off, I'll be on my way. Did things go okay, again today? Did some more of the pups find forever homes?" Jamie asked as she opened the closet to remove her winter jacket.

"Yes, some of them did. I'll tell you all about it when you get here." Ali happily replied.

"I can hear the thundering of your brother's footsteps coming down the stairs, so we'll be heading out the door in a few minutes."

"K, Mom. Susan said she's looking forward to being able to say hello, too. See you soon." Ali said as she disconnected the call and turned to help Susan lift kennels out of the back of the van.

"I'll carry Lucy and Rascal's kennels in and I'll be right back out to help you unload the larger ones, Susan."

"Thanks, Ali. I know I say this off and on, but I don't know what I'd do without all of your help!" Susan said as she hopped up into the van to pull more kennels toward the back doors.

"I don't know what I'd do without these rescues in my life, Susan. I'm really excited about my Mom getting a chance to finally meet Lucy face to face. I'm hoping that she will fall in love before I 'pop the question' again." Ali said as she carried the two smaller kennels into the house.

"Just make sure your Mom knows that I'm not the one who put you up to things, Ok?" Susan asked as she stepped down out of the van, setting one of the medium sized kennels onto the driveway, behind the van.

"Definitely! She knows that I never need anyone to prod me when it comes to animals." Ali replied with a broad smile.

"So…this is little Lucy, who you've been non-stop talking about for the past few weeks?" Jamie asked, as she bent down to say hello to the little black dog who was dancing around at their feet. "I can definitely see why she's stolen your heart!"

As Lucy stood onto her hind legs, she raised her front paws up toward Jamie, who immediately picked her up. As she pulled her close, Lucy quickly covered Jamie's chin with wet doggy kisses. It was as if Lucy knew that she needed to win Jamie over.

"And, Mom, this is Rascal. He's the deaf one that I told you about. I want you to watch what he can do. I've been teaching him sign language."

Lucy settled herself into Jamie's arms and silently turned her head to look down at Rascal. Jamie gently laid her chin on top of the little dog's head, and inhaled the scent of the shampoo that had been used to bathe Lucy the day before.

As Ali gently tapped Rascal on his shoulder, the little golden dog looked up into her eyes. Ali held her hand up where he could see it, and motioned downward, silently asking him to sit. Rascal blinked a couple of times and then sat down, never taking his eyes off of Ali.

"Good boy, Rascal!" Ali praised the little dog, despite his lack of hearing, and then motioned with her hand, palm up, while curling her fingers toward her, signaling for him to come and follow her.

Rascal promptly stood and began to walk towards Ali. Ali continued the hand signal and as she walked, he followed at her heels. When she dropped her hand to her side, Rascal stopped and waited for the next signal. Ali bent down, held her hand in front of his face, palm toward him with fingers pointing up and asked him to stay. Ali then turned to walk away from him. Rascal made no move as he patiently stood, waiting for the next sign. As soon as Ali motioned him to come, he quickly ran to her and gave a happy little bark when she bent to pet his fuzzy head.

The final sign Ali demonstrated was to gently slapping her hand down onto the floor. Rascal quickly complied by lying down onto his stomach and surprised even Ali when he lay down onto his side and then, rolled over. As he stood to shake off, he had Susan, Jamie and Alison all laughing. Since Lucy didn't seem to approve of Rascal stealing the show, she began to bark and squirmed around, wanting to get down. As Jamie set her onto the floor, Lucy ran into Alison's loving arms and smothered her face with more of her wet doggy kisses.

"My goodness, Ali, I didn't realize that Rascal was getting so good at signing!" Susan said, as she bent down to give Rascal a gentle scratch behind his ears.

"He's so smart, Susan. I was sure that he'd find a family today." Ali's voice conveyed the sadness that she was feeling.

"So, no one wanted to adopt him…again?" Jamie asked. "What about little Lucy…did she find a home, so that she'll be leaving here soon?"

"Sadly, Rascal spent most of the morning in one of the pens," Susan replied, "People are hesitant to take home the older dogs. I don't think it's his deafness as much as it is his age that kept people away. Even Lucy was being carried around by another couple who had beel looking for a small dog, but they decided against it when they were told her age. This is the second time that she came really close to finding a home. I don't blame people for not wanting the older dogs, some of them are afraid that they could be adopting a lot of health issues, due to the advanced age of the dog. To me, my dogs have always been like family. I guess that's why I can't understand how it is that so many dogs end up being surrendered every year."

"I can't either," Jamie thoughtfully replied, "it seems like once they become a part of a family, it would be terribly painful to let them go."

"Mom…which causes me to pose a question to you…" Ali's trepidation crept into her voice, "I know that I already hinted around about the fact that I wanted to bring Rascal and Lucy home to live and I know that our move played a big role in your answer…"

Jamie looked into the face of her daughter, knowing what was coming next. "And…?"

"Mom, please don't be angry with me, but I took it upon myself to ask our landlord if we could have a pet…No, wait, Mom," she said as she saw the look that quickly came over her mother's face "…it was because I met one of the other families and they were walking their dog…anyway, the landlord said that we can have *one* pet…I really didn't go behind your back, he was outside one day, changing a handle on one of the exterior faucets."

"Thank you for not deliberately going behind my back." Jamie replied, reading the worry in her daughter's face as Susan quietly tip-toed away from the conversation that was taking place, carrying Rascal in her arms.

It was at that moment that Lucy turned toward Jamie and reached her paws out, 'asking' Ali to let her go back into the arms of her mom. As Jamie looked into the big brown eyes of the little dog, she was suddenly smitten and couldn't stop a smile from making its way onto her face. Ali stood silently as Jamie once again, took the little dog into her arms, accepting additional wet kisses to be slathered onto her chin.

As Jamie looked from Lucy to Ali, her resolve was broken by the pleading look on her dear daughter's face. "Okay…so, what are the next steps that we need to take, in order to give this little dog a home?"

Alison stood mutely watching, as her mother snuggled the little black dog. She was unsure if she had heard correctly, but as her mother's words began to sink in, Ali let out a whoop as she wrapped her arms around both mother and dog.

"Are you serious? I can't believe it! I've already saved everything that we'll need to pay for the pet deposit…I promise I'll take really good care of Lucy…Ty is going to be so excited! He told me that all he'd like for Christmas this year is a dog… Is this really happening? Lucy… Lucy! You're coming home with us! Lucy, you're coming home!"

"Ali…stop…for a minute! Take a breath! You're squishing Lucy and me!" Jamie's happy request of her daughter finally got Alison to stop squeezing the air out of them.

"Susan!" Alison called.

"I know, Ali, I couldn't help but overhear!" Susan said laughingly as she came back into the room.

It was when Rascal walked in, following closely at Susan's heels, that Alison's countenance immediately changed from one of exuberance, to that of sadness. As Ali bent over to take him into her arms, her tears began to flow. Tears of happiness mixed with those of sadness, as she cuddled the little blonde dog.

"Rascal," she whispered into his fur, "I wanted both of you, but I just can't, the landlord won't let me…I promise I'll bring Lucy to see you every time I come. I know how much you've grown to love her. I also know that one day there will be a perfect home for you, too. But for now, I get to keep on loving you until you get your forever home."

As Jamie and Susan listened to Alison's sweetly whispered words, they couldn't stop their own tears from falling. Even Lucy was completely silent as she observed the touching scene taking place between Alison and her pal, Rascal. The little dog wasn't sure what was ahead. All she knew is that she felt safe in the security of Jamie's arms.

Chapter Twenty-one

As Jamie walked into the high school, she heard the sound of rapidly approaching footsteps coming up behind her.

"Yoo hoo…Jamie!" she heard Sharon's voice, requesting her attention. As she turned to face her friend, Sharon's sweater couldn't help but bring a smile to her face.

"Are you going for the ugly Christmas sweater look today?" Jamie asked, as she giggled at the sight of a blinking nose on a giant reindeer head that covered the entire front of the sweater.

"Well! If you weren't my best friend, I'd be offended!" came Sharon's giggled reply. "I found this on a clearance table after Christmas last year…it was only three dollars! Even though it's rather brash, I knew my kids would get a big kick out of it!"

Sharon's eclectic taste in clothing was something that Jamie had always admired. She had often wished that she'd been born with the same courage that was manifested in her friend's unconventional wardrobe choices. Since Sharon taught the high school's special education classes, she always dressed in a manner that helped her students to feel accepted. And they did.

Sharon loved her job, going above and beyond when it came to the kids who attended her classroom. She wasn't there for the sake of a job, she was there to serve a slice of the population who she felt deserved all the same respect that all of the other students did. Sharon always went the extra mile for 'her kids', making sure that they received every opportunity available to them, based on their skill levels. It wasn't just the special education students who adored

Sharon and her very welcoming wardrobe; she was beloved by students from every walk of life. 'Brains, nerds, jocks', the list went on. Both she and Jamie were some of the teachers whose advice was sought for a number of the day's current problems. Their love for the students was obvious, and it was that love that continued to bring a steady stream of kids to their classroom doors, before and after school.

"Anyway, enough about my wardrobe…how is Lucy settling into the household? Remember, I told you…it was only a matter of time!"

"I know, you got that right. My resolve was destroyed when I looked into the eyes of that little dog and into the face of my daughter. How was I supposed to say 'no' to that?"

"I knew you'd cave, you're such a softie when it comes to your kids…and rightly so, because you're privileged to be raising two very wonderful kids!"

"I am, Sharon. I'm so blessed. I wish that Matt was here to see what great kids we have." Jamie quietly replied.

"I have no doubt whatsoever that he knows. I feel sure that there are windows in heaven and every so often, they get to take a look at what's going on down here. And Matt probably takes a look more frequently than a lot of other folks 'up there'."

"Anyway," Jamie spoke again, "little Lucy is such a joy. Tyler and Ali absolutely adore her and she seems to be doing really well at sharing her canine love equally, and with not just the kids. She always tries to make some time for me, too."

"She's so adorable, Alison texted me some pictures." Sharon replied. "She almost makes me want to add a dog to my own life."

"Do you really think that Tigger would allow a dog into 'his' house?" Jamie asked, referring to Sharon's cross-eyed half Siamese, and half who knew what else, because Tigger had also been a rescue.

"Yah, no, you're right. He definitely rules the roost. At times, I'm surprised that he allows *me* to be a part of his life!" Sharon laughed. "Have you discovered if Lucy has any bad habits while she's been adjusting?"

"No, Sharon, I'm so amazed at how well she's fit into the family. She's housebroken and hasn't had any accidents yet, which is wonderful! We've finally found a small kibble that she seems to really like so she's eating better. In fact, I don't think it was the food that she originally rebelled against; I think it was all of the changes that the poor little thing had gone through."

"So, no problems…a great dog to go with great kids, in a great family! She's one lucky little dog." Sharon replied with a smile.

"There are just a few things that I don't quite understand about our new little family member."

"And, what would those be?" Sharon asked.

"Well, the other evening, while the kids were outside visiting with some of the neighbors, I heard another crash at the intersection of Bryant and Stone. I swear, that intersection is one of the worst ones in this town and I think it's because people come rushing down the hill on Bryant, trying to make it through the light at Stone."

"I've just about gotten hit at that intersection! It's downright dangerous! But now, getting back to the subject of Lucy…what happened?" Sharon asked.

"Shortly after hearing the crash, per usual, I heard the sirens, and Lucy went crazy! She started running around in circles while frantically barking and screeching. She seemed terrified. Then she ran over to me, wanting me to pick her up and after I did, she wrapped her little paws around my neck, like she was trying to keep me from going anywhere. Her little heart was beating about ninety miles an hour and she was quivering! She was absolutely terrified and wouldn't settle down until the sirens stopped."

"Wow, I wonder what the problem was? Maybe it was just the sound bothering her ears?" Sharon said as she pondered what she had just been told.

"Yah, maybe, but it seemed to be more than that. When I told Ali about it, she said that something similar had happened when Lucy was staying at the Rescue. I guess a police cruiser was running its sirens while pulling over a speeder. Lucy screeched and wrapped herself around Ali's leg until she picked her up and then she wrapped her paws around her neck, just like she did with me. Maybe you're right, maybe she has a problem of some kind and the sound of sirens is just too much for her little ears. Other than that, she's fit into the family just fine, as long as she has her scarf, she's perfectly content."

"Her scarf?" Sharon asked, perplexed. "Like, she's really interested in fashion or something like that? Because I'd definitely like a dog that was into fashion!"

"Nope, definitely not Lucy! She hates clothing of any kind! She came with a man's neck scarf that she drags around like it's a security blanket. If any of us tries to take it from her, she clamps her little teeth onto it and gives us 'the look'. Like she dares us to try and take it away from her. Ali said that they didn't allow her to take it to the Meet and Greets because she's been known to growl at any of the other dogs who dare to even so much as look at her precious scarf!"

"Sounds like you have a little dog with a few issues. Abandonment can do that to an animal. After all, Tigger came with his own emotional baggage and I always thought that cats were so aloof that they wouldn't possibly have any issues! Is there anything else that you've begun to notice about Lucy?"

"Well, there is one other thing that's a little peculiar. Whenever I've taken her out for a walk …she seems to really like men!"

"Oh, that sounds like a good thing! I might have to borrow her one of these days, especially if she's into meeting men!" Sharon laughingly replied.

"No, you wouldn't want to borrow her, because she only seems to like *older* men. Like, a *lot* older, as in, she seems to prefer gray haired men! And Ali has said that she's noticed the same thing. Whenever Lucy saw older men at the meet and greets, she seemed desperate to be able to get to them and after she managed to get their attention…which she easily does with that shrill little bark of hers...after 'checking them out' she always wanted down, so that she could just walk away and go back to Ali."

"Well, that doesn't seem like such a bad thing."

"No, it's not. But whenever a man gets down to her level, and she gets a good look at his face, she seems to lose all interest. It's like Lucy is looking for someone."

"Maybe she used to be owned by an older man." Sharon had just begun to open her mouth to say something more, when the bell rang, "And now, I'm off to entertain my students with this blinking sweater!" she said with a wink of her eye.

Jamie shook her head, smiled and waved at her friend, as she rose to go and greet the students who began streaming into her classroom.

Chapter Twenty-two

"Travis, are you able to take a call on line one?" The voice of his secretary came over the phone's intercom.

"Thank you, Rosemary, yes; I've got a few minutes before my next appointment." He replied as he picked up the receiver.

"Hello. Is this Mr. Travis Redman?" a young male voice asked.

"Yes, it is. May I ask who is calling?"

"Sir, my name is Daniel and I'm calling from the shelter that you visited last week."

"Oh, yes. Daniel! I'm so happy to take your call and I'm really hoping that you can help me to find a missing dog named Lucy." Travis excitedly replied.

"Josie had told me about your visit and that she had given you a little information when you were getting ready to leave. After looking at Lucy's files, I wanted to be sure that Josie was correct with the information that she had given you. And I'm happy to tell you that she was."

"Oh my, oh gosh, I can't tell you what good news you've just given me! I'm just so thankful that she wasn't euthanized!"

"No, sir, she wasn't euthanized. A woman named Susan, from the Misfit Rescue came in to meet her almost as soon as she had been brought into the shelter. Lucy was chipped, so using the chip information that was in her file, I've looked online to see if she has been registered to a new owner."

"And…?" Travis asked.

"Currently, it's not showing that anyone has updated her information, so she probably hasn't been adopted yet and is more than likely being held at the Rescue. I tried to call Susan, but since she works a full-time job to help cover the expenses of her dog rescue, she won't be home until this evening."

"Is there any way that you can provide me with her contact information? But I wouldn't want you to give me information unless you have permission to do so." The lawyer in him spoke.

"It's okay; I can give you her information so that you can call her. She's generous when it comes to that because she's always hoping for contacts that are interested in adopting or who possibly want to get involved in one way or another. Besides, Josie vouched for you, so I'm happy to give you Susan's information…have you got a pen?"

As Travis hung up the phone, he felt ecstatic about the strong possibility that he had found Lucy. He had been carrying a burden ever since he'd found out that John's little dog had been surrendered. John had trusted him and Travis had felt like he'd let him down. He could hardly wait for the day to end so that he could give Susan a call and make arrangements to pay a visit to the Misfit Rescue in the morning.

"Rosemary?" he asked, as he pushed the intercom button on his phone.

"Yes?" his secretary answered.

"Would you mind moving my schedule for tomorrow morning around a bit? I might be coming in to work a little late."

"That won't be a problem, Travis. Your first appointment tomorrow isn't until 11:00. Will that give you enough time?"

"Oh, that's right; I had forgotten that my 9:00 had to cancel. Eleven should be just fine." Travis replied, as he looked down at the information that he had gotten from Daniel and did some quick time and mileage calculations in his head. "Thank you. I should easily be able to be in the office by then."

After hanging up the phone, Susan let out a deep sigh. The call that she had just taken wasn't going to bode well for Ali. This was a conundrum and there wasn't going to be an easy answer for either side of the problem. As Bailey, Susan's basset hound, looked up at her with his big, brown eyes, she wondered if he had any idea of the sadness that she was feeling. If she wasn't so tired from a long day at work, she might have spent more time stressing over it. But tomorrow was another day, today had enough problems of its own. A good night's sleep would benefit her far more than worrying about the meeting that she was going to have in the morning.

"C'mon, Bailey and Rascal. The pups are all tucked in, so let's head off to bed." Susan said, as she headed down the hallway, with both dogs following closely on her heels.

Susan had just finished feeding all of the dogs, when she heard a soft knock at her door, resulting in a barrage of barking from the canines who all felt that it was their job to announce anyone who came to visit. She was glad that she had just closed the gate, keeping them from following her to the door, but allowing them to observe what was going on. Her stern "Hush!" amazingly, quieted most of them.

As she opened the door, Bailey and Rascal stood protectively beside her. As she looked into the eyes of the man that she had spoken to on the phone last evening, she couldn't help but notice the kindness that she saw there. His face lit up in a smile as he reached out his hand towards her.

"Good morning. You must be Susan?" Travis said, as he shook her hand.

"And, I take it that you must be Travis." Susan smiled, hoping that it could help to cover the trepidation that she was feeling.

"And who are these little furry critters?" Travis asked as he knelt down onto one knee and cautiously reached out a hand towards Bailey and Rascal.

"You might want to get your knee off the floor or you'll probably have a pretty hairy pants leg if you don't." She said as she noticed the dark navy suit that he was wearing.

"It's okay. A little dog hair never scared me. I've found that a little bit of tape usually takes it off." He said as he began to scratch Bailey behind the ear. "Is this ok? I probably should have asked before I tried to pet your dogs."

"It's fine, these two are both friendly and love any extra attention that they can get."

"And, what's your name?" Travis asked as he switched from scratching Bailey to rubbing the top of Rascal's fuzzy blonde head.

"He's Rascal…he's deaf and he's older, but I'm definitely glad that we rescued him because he's a real sweetheart." Susan proudly replied.

As Travis cupped Rascal's head in his hands, rubbing him just below the ears, the little dog had a hard time keeping his eyes open as he relished the gentle massage. "You look exactly like a little dog that I had when I was a boy. His name was B.J. It stood for 'Be Joyful'. He was my whole world when my parents gave him to me on my tenth birthday. In fact, one of the hardest days of my life was when I had to leave him with my folks when I left for college. But he joined me in my bachelor pad during my second year of college. Then came the most difficult day of all, the day I had to say good-bye forever. It was so painful that I couldn't bring myself to try to replace him with another dog. Shortly after that, I enlisted, so there was no way for me to fit another dog into my life. I think it might have been for the best. No other dog could have replaced B.J."

"Have you had any dogs since him?" Susan curiously asked.

"No, I haven't. Once B.J. was gone, college and my career became too consuming and I didn't want to have to leave a dog unattended at home for so many hours every day. It's only been the last few years that I feel like I've had some time for doing things other than working day and night."

As he stood, Rascal took a step forward and leaned his head on Travis's shin, rubbing his head up and down, as if he hadn't been ready for his massage to come to an end. Travis looked down and laughed, getting down onto both knees and resuming the gentle strokes to his ears.

Susan watched with a hopeful smile on her face, before asking, "Have you ever thought of taking a rescued dog home with you?"

As Travis looked up, she noticed a tear in one of his eyes. "You know, Susan, I was just thinking that it's really tempting to take some time to think about making this little guy a part of my life. I have enough freedom in my schedule now that I could check in on him during the day and I spend most of my evenings at home, not doing much of anything anyway."

"Remember, he's older, though," Susan replied, "but when the vet checked him out, he said he's in pretty good health. And he's really smart and has been learning different signs really quickly. Ali, one of my volunteers, has been teaching him. In fact, Ali is the one whose mother gave her permission to give a 'forever home' to your little Lucy this past weekend. Which brings me to the next question, after speaking to you last evening, it sounds like you will have to take possession of Lucy again? Because it was a stipulation in the will, is that correct?"

"Yes, the will was very specific when it came to all things, regarding Lucy. I was supposed to take and keep possession of Lucy until the reading of the will, after which, my parents would be taking permanent 'custody'. They have always loved little Lucy and she knows them. She belonged to my dad's best friend and they had made these arrangements just before he died. I'm a part of the back-up plan, and am the one who will be handling everything for her. But I assure you, when Lucy moves in with my parents they will give the little dog a wonderful home. She'll never lack for the love that John wanted her to have."

"This is all so hard." Susan sighed deeply. "Alison lost her dad a little more than a year ago. She had fallen head over heels for several of the rescues during her time here, as a volunteer. Since their rental agreement only allowed them to have one pet, she had finally decided on Lucy. I don't know how she's going to handle another loss."

Travis listened carefully as he continued to stroke both Rascal and Bailey. "I don't know what to say. I have an iron clad obligation to fulfill my client's wishes, but it sounds like Lucy has already found a very caring home."

As Travis stood, Susan noticed his two very hairy knees and had to stifle a laugh. "I completely understand. The arrangements that have been made aren't just from a legal standpoint, but even more so, it sounds to me that they were arranged based upon a trusted friendship. Do you think it would be possible for Ali to have visitation rights?"

"I feel sure that my parents would be more than willing to allow visitation." Travis replied as he attempted to wipe a few hairs off the knees of his trousers. "And Susan, I'm not going to ask you to be the 'bad guy' in all of this. Please, let me visit the family and talk to all of them. I've had a lot of experience in matters like this and I promise you, I'll be very gentle. I'll first speak to Ali's mother and get her input on how to approach her daughter and son."

"That will be fine with me." Susan replied, wiping tears from her eyes. "In fact, this week is extremely busy for both Ali and Ty. It's the last week of school before Christmas break, so Ali will be studying for semester finals and won't have the time to volunteer for me at all, this week. She can't attend Saturday's meet and greet either, because she's helping to decorate for her school's upcoming Christmas dance next week. She'll finally be back in to volunteer the following week, so at least I won't have to try to avoid her. She's a pretty perceptive little gal and she'd catch on immediately and suspect that something was wrong."

"Meet and greet?" Travis asked.

"We take some of the rescues in to the pet stores on Saturday mornings. It gives people an opportunity to meet some of the dogs and help them to decide if they're interested in adoption."

"Ah, I see, thus the name, 'Meet and Greet'. And Susan, I promise that I'll be very gentle in the way that I handle this situation with Alison's family. I'll take the utmost care to ensure that everyone can come out feeling like a winner, when it comes to Lucy's placement." Travis's reassuring tone helped to set Susan's mind at ease. "In the meantime, what does one have to do, in order to adopt one of your dogs? If it's all right with you, I'd like to give little Rascal a forever home. It's time for me to have more in my life than just my career."

Chapter Twenty-three

As Ty sat at the breakfast bar, working on homework, he heard the doorbell ring. "I'll get it, Ali." He yelled up the stairs to his sister, "Since Mom's not home, I'll be sure to look through the peephole before I open the door."

"Good idea!" she yelled back down the stairs.

As Ty stood onto his tip toes to see who was at the door, quickly shook his head, as if to clear his mind, before looking again and finally opening the door.

"Gramma?...and Grampa?" he asked incredulously. "What are you *doing* here? Mom's not home right now, but she should be here any minute."

As he continued to stare with saucer sized eyes, he heard Ali yell, "Who is it, Ty?"

"I think you'd better come down here, Ali!"

"Why? I'm in the middle of studying for a big test!" she yelled back to her brother.

"I really think you need to come down here!"

As Ali began to come down the stairs, Ty could hear her feet stomp on each step, letting him know that she was angry for having to come down the stairs at all. As she finally reached the living room, she looked down the stairs to the entryway, where Ty stood with their grandparents. As Ali's mouth dropped open, there was no question about her surprise at their presence.

"Grampa!...and Gramma!" What are *you* doing here?" not realizing that she had echoed her brother's previous question, eventually coming the rest of the way down the stairs to wrap her arms around the grandparents that she hadn't seen in over a year.

As her grandparents pulled both Ali and Ty into their arms, all four of them began to sob uncontrollably.

"Can you kids ever forgive us?" they heard their Grandmother ask.

"We're so very, very sorry." Their grandfather added.

As they all continued to hold one another, none of them noticed the sound of the garage door being opened. When Jamie came in from the garage, she found a huddle of four, all of them still crying.

"What on earth?" she asked, surveying the scene before her, repeating the same question that they had already heard twice before. "What are you doing here? And, please, come upstairs where we'll all have a little more room than we do down here!"

As everyone finally let go of each other, using hands to dry their eyes, they all headed up the stairs to the living room and sat down.

As Matt's dad, Rich, turned to Jamie and softly spoke. "We're so sorry. Can you ever forgive us?"

Instead of answering, Jamie asked, "How did you find us?"

It was Matt's mother, Nancy who spoke up, "We got your Christmas letter and we wanted to write you back, to ask you if we could come and see all of you, but we were afraid that you'd say no."

"So we decided we'd just come, without an invitation, because we wanted to see everyone again. So, here we are…and we're hoping that you won't throw us out." Rich added.

"Never, we're not going to throw you out, but you have to realize that we're really confused by your unexpected visit. We haven't even seen you since Matt's service. I thought that maybe you've been angry with me…I thought that perhaps, you blamed me for not doing enough, or something…I didn't know. We haven't seen a whole lot of either of you over the years, you were always traveling…so, I…I'm sorry for not being able to make myself very clear in what I'm trying to say."

"Oh, Jamie, it's nothing that you did or didn't do. It's us; all of this has been our fault and we're so ashamed to have missed out on so much of your lives…on our son's life, and now, it's too late! We were too late! We always thought that we'd have more time, but time just slipped away." Nancy said, as she laid her head into her palms and began to sob.

"Right around the time you and Matt were married, we hit the big time. You remember, don't you?" Rich began to explain. "Our business had finally taken off and after years of struggling, when a large corporation saw the potential in what we had initiated, they bought us out. Suddenly we had more money than we'd ever dreamed we'd have. We tried to give Matt some of our money to make your lives easier, but you know him. He was determined to make it in life with no help from anyone…and then we got busy. We were finally able to travel anywhere, so we did."

"We thought we'd have plenty of years left to make up for lost time. But it wasn't to be. And all the money in the world can't undo the mistakes that we made." Nancy said as she looked at the tearful faces of her grandchildren, who had been intently listening to everything that had just been said. "And we had enough money that we could have helped Matt, if we had known how sick he was."

"It all happened so fast, everything progressed so fast. I had even mortgaged the house in order to pay for the only hope they offered…an experimental treatment that didn't produce the results that everyone had hoped for…and then, in a matter of weeks, it was over. I'm sorry if you thought that we tried to keep things from you. We had no idea what we were up against, Matt fought as hard as he could, but the treatments didn't work…" Jamie stopped to wipe at her own tear streaked face.

"Oh Jamie, we had no idea, we had thought that maybe Matt hadn't been telling us what was going on…we thought that maybe he didn't want to interrupt our travels…" Nancy said as she dug in her purse for a tissue. "We're just so sorry that we didn't make the time for *all* of you. We haven't been traveling, ever since coming here for Matt's service. We've been at home, grieving everything that our negligence caused us to miss out on. We…we want to make some changes to our lives…"

"Nancy and I are hoping that the three of you can find it in your hearts to allow us to come back into your lives. We'd give anything to be able to spend time with all of you, if you can just, please, forgive us."

After rising from her seat, Jamie stood silently for a moment before crossing the room to put her arms around the two people that she had never stopped caring about; the two people who had, in the early days of marriage, begun to fill the void caused by the absence of her own parents. As Ali and Ty stood the place their arms around them, everyone began to find comfort in the warm embraces of one other. In the arms of their family, both Rich and Nancy had begun to find the unconditional love and forgiveness that they had long desired.

"Why don't we head to the table and I'll make us all something to eat." Jamie said as she rose from her chair in the living room.

"Oh no, we don't want to be a bother, you don't need to make us anything." Nancy said as she followed Jamie into the kitchen.

"You're not a bother. I can guarantee that any minute Ty is going to ask me if there's anything to eat. He's growing like a weed and his body seems to need more fuel than anyone I've ever known."

"Why don't you let Rich and I order pizza for all of us?"

"Gramma, that sounds great!" Ty said, overhearing the conversation. "Mom probably already told you that food and I get along *really* well these days."

"Yes she did, Ty, so why don't you and Alison decide what kind pizzas we should order, so we can feed two growing teenagers! Or, I should actually say, one growing teenage girl and her hungry younger brother!"

When the pizza delivery man rang the doorbell, the sound must have awakened Lucy from a long overdue nap that she had been taking on the bed in Ali's room. Barking frantically, she came running down the stairs at amazing speed. As she ran to the front door, she didn't pay any attention to the two extra strangers in the house. While Ty paid for the pizza with the money from his Grandpa, Lucy sat at his feet, sniffing the air. As Ty came up the stairs, Lucy followed on his heels, not even bothering to bark at Rich or Nancy.

"Oh my, and who are you?" Nancy asked, looking down at the little black dog who was staring at the pizza boxes that Ty held in his hands.

"That's Lucy, Gramma." Ali informed her, as she bent over to scoop Lucy into her arms. "She's the newest member of our family. I got her from the rescue home where I volunteer. I'll fill you in while we eat our pizza."

While gathered around the small table, after filling up on pizza, they spent the rest of the evening catching up on one another's lives. Lucy had gone from Nancy to Rich and back again, making fast friends with both of them, especially after she'd received some tidbits from their hands.

Eventually, as Rich looked over at his wife, he said, "We should be going; you probably all need to be up early in the morning." We have a room for tonight, at a motel that's not far from here, and we should probably check in soon, or they might think that we're not coming."

"Grampa, you'll be back, won't you?" Ty asked, with a concerned look on his face.

"Absolutely, Ty, we'll be back often. After all, we're only a short flight away." Rich said, wiping a tear from the corner of his eye.

"And Grampa and I want you to send us a schedule of special school events. We want to be a part of *everything*!" Nancy said, before turning to her daughter-in-law, "Jamie, if there's ever anything that we can do to help you in any way, please, let us know. We're so thankful that you've let us back into your lives and we want to promise you that things will be different from now on."

"Maybe next year, we can start a new tradition, by celebrating together." Rich's voice sounded hopeful. "This year we're going to be at my brother's; his health is beginning to fail and we have many 'fences to mend' with others, too."

"Next year." Jamie said as she smiled at her in-laws.

As everyone rose from the table, they gathered together once again for another warm embrace. While the good-byes were tearful, they weren't tears of sadness, instead, of joy, and the hopeful anticipation of new beginnings.

Chapter Twenty-four

As Travis and Susan finished up all of the adoption paperwork, he couldn't help but wonder if adopting a dog was going to be a good idea. He had weighed the pros and cons, and his primary hesitance had been the fact that he had to be at the office every day and hoped that his new pet wasn't going to be too lonely, after having so many other dogs to keep him company.

It was as if Susan read his mind, when she looked at him and asked, "Are you having second thoughts, after taking just two days to think about adopting Rascal?"

"No second thoughts about taking Rascal home, I'm just hoping that he's going to be okay with it. He seems to be rather attached to you and he never lacks for companionship here. I'm going to be taking him home to an empty bachelor pad and the poor little guy is going to have to spend the majority of his day on his own. Do you think he'll be okay?"

"Rascal's had a hard time being here. With his profound deafness, he's not always sure of what's going on around him when the other dogs all get worked up about something. The poor little guy has been run over by some of the larger dogs, because he couldn't hear them coming. I tend to keep him and my own dog, Bailey, away from the other dogs, while they hang with me. As a result, he's begun to attach himself to me."

"That's my concern. He's already been abandoned once, I'm afraid that he's really going to miss you and wonder what's happening to him again."

"This is, unfortunately, part of what happens to rescue dogs. They first have to accept the loss of the families that they loved. Then they go into my home, or the homes of one of the other foster families, where they tend to get attached, only to learn that they will have to go through another loss when they're finally adopted into a forever home."

"It just seems like it's so unfair to these animals. It's truly, heartbreaking." Travis said as he sadly looked into Susan's eyes, revealing a sadness all their own.

"I know. That's why I began rescuing these dogs in the first place. I just wanted some of them to get a second chance to know what it was like to be accepted once again, and learn to love and be loved. We have so many wonderful success stories."

"Do the rescued dogs usually end up going to really good homes?" Travis asked.

"Almost all of them do. Every once in a while, an adoption doesn't work out as we had hoped, but those situations are few and far between. The majority are success stories because the people who've decided to adopt tend to be really committed to taking in a rescue, instead of a new puppy."

"Thanks, Susan. Everything you've just shared has helped me to realize that I definitely want to go ahead with Rascal's adoption. Since I don't have to put in as many hours at the office as I used to, I should have sufficient time to spend with him so he won't feel too lonely."

"I think you're going to find that he'll be perfectly content to be an 'only dog'. Because he's older, he really likes to sleep; once he gets away from the chaos of my home, he'll probably try to catch up on some much needed naps!"

"After a rough week in court, I'll probably be right there next to him, catching up on some sleep of my own!" Travis said with a grin.

"Okay now, here are your copies of his paperwork and this harness and leash are his to keep. I've also got a baggie of the dog food that he's been eating while he's been here. The note taped to the side of it tells you what kind it is. It's always best to keep them on the same diet so that they don't get an upset stomach. If you decide to change his food to something else, please do so slowly. That way it won't be such a shock to his system. And Travis…please feel free to call me anytime with any questions or concerns that you might have. I'm here to support all of my new adoptive 'parents'." Susan laughed as she began putting everything into a small cloth bag with the Misfit Rescue logo on the front.

"Oh, and also, he knows a little bit of sign. Here, let me show you some of the basics." She said and proceeded to give him a quick demonstration. "Hand out in front, if you curl your fingers toward you, he knows he's supposed to come. Hand up, in the stop position lets him know that you want him to stay. Slapping your hand lightly onto the floor usually results in him lying down…but, not always. Sometimes, he has his own agenda."

After finishing up all of the verbal instructions and handing the bag to Travis, Susan got down onto her knees in front of Rascal, and with tears in her eyes, she hugged him goodbye.

As Travis looked over to his new charge that was lying silently on the bucket seat beside him, he said, "Hey, old boy, don't look so sad. I'm going to give you a lot of love and I hope that you'll learn to love me, too."

He slowly reached across the console to pet Rascal's soft head. The small dog's eyes looked up at him, but he continued to keep his head down between his paws. As soon as Travis stopped petting him, he turned his head away and looked over towards the door.

"You poor little guy. It must have been hard being left at a shelter, especially being deaf. You weren't able to even hear them tell you goodbye, so I'm sure you had a really hard time trying to understand what was happening. Well, never again, Rascal. You're going to be with me until the end and I hope that one day, you'll learn to trust again."

As Travis finished the drive home and turned the corner to pull onto his own street, he noticed his parents' car parked in the driveway. "Oh good, Rascal. My parents are going to get to meet their new grand-dog! Talk about a surprise after all the times that I've told them 'no more dogs'! I bet they're going to learn to love you, just like they did my old dog, B.J. And, in a few days, you'll probably perk up when you get to see Lucy again…hopefully. I heard that you and little Lucy used to be good friends. I'm pretty sure that's why the folks are here. They want to know when I'll be picking Lucy up, old boy."

As he pulled carefully past his parents' car and into the garage, Rascal suddenly sat up, trying to gather information by looking out the window of the car.

When Travis walked into his home leading Rascal, who gingerly stepped through the door, unsure of whether or not he should even enter the house.

"And who is this?" Travis's mom asked, as soon as she saw the little dog follow Travis into the living room, where Mary and David had been sitting and watching the news on t.v.

"This…is Rascal. Say hello to your new grand-dog!" Travis introduced him with a smirk on his face.

"He reminds me of B.J." David said as he rose from the couch to get a better look at Rascal.

"That's why I decided to adopt him, because he reminded me so much of old B.J."

"I thought you said that you were never going to get another dog."

"I know, Mom; I felt like I'd never want another dog, but since my life has finally settled down to a 'dull roar', I decided that it would be okay to give this little guy a permanent home."

"I assume that he must have been living at the rescue place, where you had finally gotten the information on what had happened to Lucy?" She asked.

"He was. He's an older dog and he's completely deaf."

"Why didn't you get something younger, and a dog who could hear?" David asked as he bent over to scratch the top of Rascal's head.

"I don't know…maybe it's because I'm always working to help the underdog. As much as I had never wanted to say good-bye to another dog, this little guy was greatly in need of a new home so I decided that I could be the one who provided it for him."

"Travis, I think it's wonderful. You spend entirely too much time alone. I think a dog will be a good companion for you."

"Thanks, Mom. I think I agree. And I'm hoping that since you and dad will be welcoming Lucy into your home, maybe we can all dog sit for one another, occasionally."

"I think that's a wonderful idea, don't you, dear?" Mary asked as she looked over to David who was still petting Rascal.

"Yes, I do. In fact, I've been wondering what we were going to do with Lucy when we decide that we want to take a trip. I figured that you'd take care of her, Travis, and now we won't have to feel guilty about doing so. Speaking of Lucy, when will you meet with the family who currently has her?"

"I'm planning on trying to meet with them on Saturday. They sound like a wonderful family. And they've all been through some grief of their own, last year. I feel really bad about all of this. I hate the fact that I feel like I'll be responsible for breaking all of their hearts again."

"I feel so bad about the way that all of this has gone, but I promised John that we'd give Lucy a home if anything ever happened to him. I had no idea that day, when we had that discussion, that we'd actually be faced with this. I was sure that John would easily outlive his little dog. I know that he felt the same way."

"It's okay, Dad, we just need to follow through to the best of our abilities, in order to honor John's wishes. And now, let me show you what this little guy can do. I'm hoping that he'll respond to me when I try to show you some of the signs that he knows."

Unfortunately, Rascal had no desire to show anyone what he could do as he stood looking blankly at Travis, who was trying to to remember the signs that Susan had shown him. Eventually, Rascal made his opinion known when he turned his back on all of them, and stubbornly sat down.

Chapter Twenty-five

Jamie had just finished tidying up the kitchen when she heard Sharon's car pull into the driveway. She was thankful that Sharon had been willing to give the kids a ride home from school, since Jamie had left early for a dental appointment. She was also glad that it was Friday and that she'd have Saturday morning to get some things done while the kids went with Sharon to decorate their school gym. Lucy quickly ditched Jamie and hurriedly ran down to the front door and sat, patiently waiting for the door to open so the kids could rumble in.

"Hi Lucy," she heard Alison say as she bent to pick up the little dog. "Oh Lucy…" Ali said as she bent her head forward to bury her face in the soft fur.

As Jamie looked at the touching scene before her, she noticed Ty's unhappy expression and held her silence as she watched Sharon put a finger to her lips, to stifle any questions that she thought Jamie might be getting ready to ask.

Ali didn't say anything as she kept her face buried in the fur of Lucy's neck. When she looked up, Jamie could see the tracks from the tears that were so obvious, on her daughter's cheeks.

"Mom, we stopped by the Rescue."

"I kind of figured that you might have, after not getting to help out all week. But what happened? Is everything okay?"

"Yes and no," Ali replied, wiping another tear from her face. "Rascal got his forever home."

"Oh, Ali, that's wonderful. I know that you're going to miss him, but he has a home in time for Christmas!"

"Mom, Susan wasn't there, so I don't have any details, but he's already gone. Jessica told me that he had been picked up the night before. Lucy didn't even get to tell him goodbye. *I* didn't get to tell him goodbye! Oh, Mom…"

Jamie quickly closed the distance between herself and her daughter and gently wrapped her arms around Ali, as she began, again, to cry. "I'm so very sorry, Ali. I know how attached you had gotten to him and I was worried that it was going to be really hard on you when he found a home."

"I'm so happy that he's got a new home, I just wish that Lucy and I had been able to tell him goodbye. Jessica said that Susan had allowed him to be adopted a little faster than what it usually takes, because she was hoping to avoid having to take him to the pet store for another 'meet and greet' tomorrow. Because of his deafness, he always seemed a little stressed out by all the comings and goings of the people who came in and out of the store. I just wish that I had been there this week and had gotten the chance to hold him one more time and tell him how much I loved him."

"Ali, he knew. Even though he was deaf, I saw how he looked at you when you were showing me all the signs that you had helped him to learn."

"Oh, Mom, I just wish that we had been able to take both of them home with us." Ali said as she reached for a tissue to wipe her face and blow her nose.

It was then that Lucy looked into Ali's eyes and let out a soft whine, as if to say that she was going to miss Rascal, too.

Both Ty and Sharon had stood silently by and watched as Jamie tenderly tried to comfort her daughter. Lucy finally turned away from Ali and looked at Ty and barked, as if she was letting him know that she needed a little comfort from him, also. As Ty reached to take Lucy from Ali's arms, she gave Ali a quick kiss on the chin and then began to rub her head on Ty's chin and neck, as if she was giving him a hug.

Once she had gotten some attention from Ty, she reached a paw toward Sharon, to let her know that it was her turn to give Lucy some loving attention.

"So, what is this?" Sharon asked as she took the little dog from Ty's arms. "Is this a game known as pass the pup?"

Lucy barked, as if to affirm that's exactly what was going on, evoking some laughter from her human audience.

"How about some hot chocolate for everyone?" Jamie asked.

"That sounds great, Mom. Have you got some cookies to go with that hot chocolate?" Ty asked, as he rubbed his hand in a circular motion over his stomach. "I'm starving!"

"Since when aren't you starving?" Sharon asked as she continued to hold and stroke Lucy.

"I guess, since never." Ty replied as he and Ali both headed for the stairs, planning to drop their back packs in their rooms and change clothes.

"I'll have it ready when you two get back down here." Jamie said, turning towards Sharon. "Thanks so much for bringing the kids home for me. You probably didn't need the drama of stopping by the Rescues, only to learn that Rascal was gone."

"Aw, it was fine. Ali just wanted to say a quick hello to the pups and let them all know that she'd be back in a few days. My heart just broke for her when I saw how upset she was that Rascal was no longer there."

As Sharon kept rubbing Lucy's head and neck, she looked down at the velvety black collar, generously sprinkled with sparkling gems. As she bent her head to look closer, she received a wet and sloppy kiss on her left cheek.

"Jamie, where did you get Lucy's collar?"

"I guess it was left on her when she was surrendered to the shelter and she was still wearing it when Susan and Ali rescued her. Susan sent it home with us, along with that neck scarf that I had already told you about and a leather leash. Why?" Jamie asked as she retrieved four cups from the kitchen cabinet and set them on the kitchen counter.

"Well, I'm definitely not an expert, but I don't think that these stones are cubic zirconia. And they're definitely not rhinestones." Sharon said as she pulled her magnifiers from her purse, enabling her to get a better look. "Actually, Jamie, I think that these might be diamonds!"

"No, they couldn't be. Who would put a diamond collar on a dog and then leave it at a shelter? That would just be crazy."

"Maybe it was someone who had no idea that they might be diamonds and figured that they were more than likely some kind of fake stones."

"No, Sharon, there's no way that those can be diamonds. Do you think?" Jamie asked.

"Again, I'm not an expert, but I did take some classes on gemology and, hmmm…" Sharon's voice trailed off as she bent closer for a better look. "I feel really sure that these aren't zirconia. The cut is suggestive of them being diamonds and I think that you should at least take this collar to a jeweler's so that an expert can take a look."

"Yah, maybe, but if that's the case, what do I do? Give them to Susan, return them to the shelter?"

"Or, you could just cash them in, keep the dough and have yourself a Merry Little Christmas. After all, it's only ten shopping days left until Christmas!" Sharon winked.

"Yah, like cashing in on someone else's mistake would be the right thing to do." Jamie replied with a smile, placing cookies onto a plate as the kids raucously descended the stairs.

"Or you could buy your best friend some really amazing Christmas sweaters off the discount rack, once the holidays are passed!"

"Which is just exactly what you need…more ugly Christmas sweaters!"

"I beg your pardon?" Sharon asked as she broke into laughter.

"I'm sorry…more of those wonderful, colorful *Christmas* sweaters! Well, if they do turn out to be diamonds, I'll make sure that you are the *first* to know."

As the kids entered the kitchen in tandem, Lucy yipped as soon as she saw Ali, who immediately took her from Sharon's arms so she could cradle her in her own.

After Sharon looked down at the caller I.D. on her phone and saw that it was from Jamie, she quickly answered, "Well, hello again! Since we haven't spoken for a few hours, did you miss me already and have to call?"

"Sharon! After you left, I went out to run a few errands. I was feeling rather curious about what you'd had to say about the stones on Lucy's collar, so I took it with me and stopped by Glenn Jewelers."

"And?"

"And, Sharon, you were right! The stones aren't cubic zirconia! They're diamonds, and he estimated the value of the stones to be worth around a thousand dollars!"

"Well then, Merry Christmas, my friend! But I know you…what are you going to do?"

"Well, for right now, Lucy is wearing a new, inexpensive collar that I picked up at the pet store and her diamond collar is locked safely inside my jewelry box, with all my cheap costume jewelry. I'll be taking it to Susan the first thing next week and let her decide how to track down the owner. Can you believe it? Who would put an expensive collar like that on a dog and then give her away?" Jamie asked.

"Her owner would have known that she was wearing a diamond collar…so it must have been someone who had no idea that the stones were diamonds. Wow! If you weren't so honest, Jamie, you could give your kids a very Merry Christmas!"

"My kids are already going to have a very Merry Christmas…Lucy was all that they wanted for Christmas this year. And I'm so thankful that we took the little dog into our home. She's infusing this Christmas season with a lot of extra love and laughter. Lucy is helping to make this Christmas less painful, as we look at celebrating our second year without Matt here, to help us. Actually,

Sharon, I think that she's been the best Christmas gift to all of us!" Jamie said as she ended the conversation and hung up the phone.

Chapter Twenty-six

As Jamie stepped out of the shower, she looked down at the newest member of her little family and smiled. "You just can't seem to take your eyes off of any of your new housemates, can you, Lucy? You'd think that after being part of our family for the past week, you'd realize that you won't be going anywhere else; this is your home. But I'm sure that you're wondering why the kids have gone somewhere, and left you behind."

Lucy cocked her head to the side and let out a small whine, bringing a smile to Jamie's face. "I'm sorry that Alison and Ty had to leave you here, all alone with just me to keep you company. They had to go help Sharon with the Christmas decorating for the upcoming school dance and there are some things that dogs just can't attend."

Lucy yipped a quick answer and followed closely behind, as Jamie left the bathroom to rifle through her dresser drawers. It didn't take long before she found the sweatshirt that had been a regular part of her Christmas apparel for a number of years.

"What do you think of this?" she asked Lucy, as she held up a red sweatshirt with the words 'HO, HO, HO' written in large white letters on the front.

Lucy stood onto her hind feet and waved her paws in the air, as if to say she thought it was a perfect selection.

"Did anyone ever tell you that you have good taste…for a dog, anyway? Oh my goodness, Lucy, if anyone hears me talking to you like I do, they're going to think I've lost a few of my marbles!"

As she finished her sentence, Jamie took the towel off her hair and pulled the sweatshirt over her head before slipping into a well-worn pair of comfortable jeans. As she walked back into the bathroom, Lucy followed closely on Jamie's heels. She sat patiently as she watched Jamie run a brush through her long, damp locks of hair, before pulling it back into a pony tail and quickly winding it into a bun at the back of her neck, in order to keep it out of her face for the task that lie ahead.

"Next stop is the kitchen, for one more cup of hot java to keep the motivation going." Jamie said, as she headed down the stairs to the main level of their tiny new abode, with Lucy hot on her trail.

The new condo was working out okay, Jamie thought to herself, as she poured a large cup of strong coffee and lightened it up with an adequate dollop of Italian sweet cream. For right now, she and Ali shared one of the two bedrooms, with Tyler across the hall in the other one. But Jamie remembered how much she had loved having her own space, back when she was a girl of Ali's age. She had wanted to let Alison have the room to herself, while Jamie had planned to sleep on the sofa, but Ali wouldn't hear of it. For the time being, the two of them crammed into a bedroom that was barely large enough for one person, let alone two people. She sighed, as she took her cup and sat down onto the comfy sofa.

Lucy immediately jumped up to snuggle beside Jamie while she drank her second and final cup of coffee for the day.

"Yep, little girl, it's just you and me for a while today." Lucy lifted her head to listen.

"Last year I didn't do any decorating for Christmas. The kids did it while I was lost in the shock of grieving…but this year, it's my turn to do the decorating." Jamie said, as she stroked the silky fur of the warm little creature beside her while savoring the taste and aroma of her coffee. "And this is perfect. We should have just enough time to get the decorations out and stand the tree up, so we can all work together on decorating it this evening."

After draining her cup, both Jamie and Lucy rose in sync and headed for the kitchen. Jamie lightly rinsed her cup and after opening up the dishwasher, she found a spot where she could nestle it into the nearly full appliance. As she added detergent and set the knob to run, Lucy finally left her side and walked over to her bowls for a final lick of her food dish before taking a drink of water.

This time it was Jamie who waited on Lucy to finish before heading down the flight of stairs that would take her out to the garage, where she could gain access into the dreaded crawl space that was tucked under the main level of the condo. Jamie had never liked crawl spaces, ever since she was a child. She thought back to that day when she and her friend, Candy, had been locked inside the one that was under Candy's house. Candy's older brother had decided to play a joke on the girls by shutting the door and sliding the glide lock closed. Jamie remembered screaming alongside Candy, as they had looked around at all the spiders that were nestled in the large web that hung precariously over their heads. Thankfully, their screams had brought Candy's mother to the rescue, where she quickly released the captives from their dark and scary surroundings. As soon as she had calmed the girls, she had left to find the son who was going to be spending some time in his room, where he could think long and hard about the dirty trick that he had played on the girls.

Jamie gave a small shudder as she shook the bad memory from her mind and reached out to open the three by three foot door, which was located in the side wall, a few feet off the garage floor. She opened up a small step ladder and centered it under the opening as she looked down at Lucy and explained, "You'll need to sit here while I crawl inside to get the decorations and the tree."

Lucy proceeded to sit down and let out a small sigh.

"You know, Lucy, I feel like you understand everything that I say to you!" to which Lucy replied with a small yip that sounded a lot like an affirmative yes.

"Well then, here I go!" Jamie said, as she mustered the courage and determination to complete the intended task.

"Seriously, Ty? What were you thinking when you crawled in here and dragged the tree so far back from the door?" Jamie muttered to herself as she walked across the dirt floor on her knees, while shining the flashlight around the darkened crawl space.

As soon as the light had revealed the plastic bag that contained the tree, her thoughts took her back to the home they had left behind and the wonderful closet under the basement stairs. It wasn't a particularly large closet. It hadn't tucked all the way back under the stairs and it had been only about three feet by three feet in size, with a slanted ceiling that came to a point at the top. Jamie and Matt had decided that there would be no need to disassemble the artificial tree any longer, after seeing a closet that appeared to have been perfectly built for storing a tree. It had enabled them to leave the tree in a standing position with all the lights still on the branches. The only thing they had needed to do after removing the ornaments was to put the tree into a plastic bag, and slide it into the closet where it had 'patiently waited' for the next Christmas celebration to come back around a year later.

But that was then, and this is now. Jamie thought as she swiped at the cob web that she felt against her cheek. So much had changed since last Christmas and even more so in the past two weeks. They had left the home that they had loved and crammed into a condo that had the total square footage of a small apartment. They had welcomed a little black dog into their lives, whose soft whimpers were letting Jamie know that she was wondering what, exactly, had happened to her new master after she'd been swallowed up by the dark hole in the garage wall.

"It's okay, Lucy. I'm okay. I'll be out in a few more minutes." Jamie said as she grasped the bag and began to drag it across the crawl space floor, which was no easy task from the stance on her knees as she ducked to keep from hitting her head on the joists located so close to her head.

Jamie heard a soft yip come from the garage as Lucy continued to impatiently wait for Jamie's return from the black hole.

"I'm almost there, Lucy." Jamie said as she backed towards the open door, dragging the tree behind her.

As soon as Lucy saw Jamie's feet coming through the opening and stepping onto the ladder, Lucy could hardly contain herself as she excitedly barked and hopped around. Once Jamie stepped off the step ladder, she shoved it aside and out of the way, as she reached in to pull the tree through the door.

Unfortunately, the plastic bag hadn't fared well during its journey through the crawl space and had sustained some large tears during its trip across the rocky dirt floor. As it was finally pulled through the opening, the bag's integrity had been so compromised that very little of the tree was still being protected by the bag. At least it had lasted long enough to keep most of the dirt off the branches.

As Jamie stood the tree onto the garage floor and assessed the damage to the bag, she decided to remove the plastic remains, knowing that it would make carrying it up the stairs a little more difficult than it would have been with the bag still in place.

Lucy sat at Jamie's feet staring at the tree, and let out a soft whine as she looked up into Jamie's face with a confused look on her little black face.

"Yep, Lucy, here's the tree. A little disheveled looking, don't you think?"

As Lucy intently listened, she cocked her head to the side before letting out a soft whine and stood onto her hind feet, asking Jamie to pick her up.

"Hang on, Lucy; I can't pick you up right now. I need to go back inside the door to get the boxes of decorations. Thankfully, Ty didn't put them all the way at the back, like he did the tree!" Jamie said as she once again disappeared from Lucy's sight, after setting the ladder back in place so that she could crawl back inside the dark cavity.

"Okay, Lucy, here come the boxes," Jamie said as she looked down at the small dog from her perch inside the dark space, "'"How I wish that I could just hand these down to you."

Lucy cocked her head to the side, before letting out a soft whine.

As Jamie emerged from the crawl space for the final time, after setting the boxes onto the garage floor, she looked back down at the little dog sitting on the floor beside her, "And now, we need to finish this task and get this beast of a tree up the stairs and into the living room."

Lucy yipped and headed for the door that led from the garage into the entryway as Jamie shook her head in disbelief, once again realizing how much human language the little dog appeared to understand. As she opened the door, Lucy ran inside the house, up the stairs and sat down at the top, finding a great vantage point for watching what came next. As Jamie held the door open, she shoved one of her boots under it in order to keep it propped open, then stepped back into the garage to get the tree.

After dragging the tree across the garage floor to the open door, Jamie squatted down and wrapped her arms around the lower part of the tree, attempting to squeeze the branches together enough to give the tree a smaller profile, for getting it up the narrow stairway to the living room. When she stood up, she realized that she had no view of where she was heading, but was thankful that she had a pretty good idea. She was also glad that she only had to climb seven steps and not a full set of stairs. Getting through the threshold was the first accomplishment as she turned sideways, still holding onto the tree, to take a quick look up the stairs before beginning her ascent from the entryway.

She carefully took one step up and had to stop when she realized that the tree had already snagged itself on the doorknob, preventing her from going any further. Once she had freed the branch, she continued blindly up the stairs as the tree managed to scrape the walls on both sides of her and seemed to attach itself to the railing and anything else that was in its vicinity. She heard the crash of one of the pictures that had previously hung near the top of the stairs, thankful that she didn't hear any breaking glass as it had taken a tumble down the stairs. She had finally reached what she thought was the top step, only to discover that she had one more to go and unfortunately, tripped over it and banged one of her knees on the edge of the step as she and the tree toppled onto the floor together. At least she was the one on top, which didn't bode well for the artificial conifer. As she and the tree both landed onto the floor, the wall at the top of the stairway had slowed the fall but it had also rearranged the shape of the tree, bending the top third over into the shape of an L.

As she rolled off the tree, Jamie leaned against the wall and began to massage her knee, realizing that the wooden threshold on the top step had dealt quite a blow to her knee cap.

"Oh, Matt…this is why I need you to be here. Some things are just too hard for me to do by myself." She said as she started to cry while rubbing her knee, as Lucy jumped onto her lap to offer her some canine comfort.

"Thank you, Lucy. I'll be okay." Jamie said as she sniffled and wiped the tears from her cheeks with her hands.

Jamie had finally calmed herself, gotten up onto her feet and was assessing her L-shaped tree when the doorbell rang.

Chapter Twenty-seven

The school auditorium was filled with teenagers, most of them wearing some kind of Christmas apparel. Some were in Santa hats and reindeer antlers. Others wore brightly colored sweatshirts and t-shirts and the ones who had forgotten to dress in something related to the season wore colorful bows, stuck on their heads, or shoulders, or shoes. Sharon and some of the other teachers had also dressed up for the occasion. It was a colorful group, all working together, as they hung red and green streamers and multiple other decorations from the ceiling and along the walls of the gymnasium. In the background, the Christmas music loudly blared, causing some of the teens to dance to the music as they congenially worked together with the other students, determined to make the place as festive as possible for the upcoming dance.

They hadn't been working for very long when a small group of parents arrived, bringing refreshments. "Come and get it!" One of the women yelled, as a hoard of teenagers dropped everything that they were doing and headed noisily for the food.

It took just a short time for the kids to move in, all of them sporting voracious appetites. By the time Sharon and the other teachers approached the tables for some sustenance of their own, they were amazed at how little had been left behind.

"Man, I feel like we just watched a band of vultures swoop in and attack the food!" Sharon said as she stood wide eyed, looking at small amount of refreshments that had been left behind.

"I agree! And, just like vultures, they seem to have picked the carcass dry!" one of the male teachers added, as the staff broke into laughter.

"You're in luck," one of the parent volunteers spoke softly; "we kept some of the goodies hidden under the table, just for you."

"Oh, bless you!" another of the staff added her opinion. "I'll run to the lounge and grab the coffee pot that I had put on earlier."

"Oh, and now, bless you!" Sharon added.

As the small crowd stood back to admire everything that they had done, they all smiled proudly, pleased with all that they had accomplished in a few short hours. The tables that had been set up along the perimeter of the gymnasium were all covered with colorful, seasonal table cloths. The kids had also scattered red, green and gold confetti, cut in Christmas-y shapes, onto the table tops. The tables had been of the utmost importance, as they would hold all of the cookies, cupcakes and drinks that would be needed to feed a large group of middle schoolers during Thursday's dance on the last day of school, before the holiday break began. The rest of the gymnasium was filled with the colors of the season, making the upcoming festivity seem that much more imminent.

The dance was a wonderful way for teachers and students, alike, to end the first half of the school year before returning in January, when they would all resume the schedule that would rapidly commence towards the completion of another year. Even though Sharon and Jamie both taught at the high school, and not the middle school, they had both been volunteering for the Christmas decorating ever since Alison had become a middle school student. Since the campuses were located so closely to one another, the staff from both schools had a great history of helping one another out for special events, and Sharon and Jamie had built good relationships with a number of the teachers who taught at the middle school.

When the final surveying of the scene before them had been completed, everyone began to say their good-byes, as parents began arriving to pick up their children. Hugs and handshakes helped to bring a close to a successful morning of decorating.

"What are you two interested in having for lunch…I'm sure that by now, Travis, you're starving, right?" Sharon asked as she and the kids buckled into their seats in her car.

"How did you ever know, Sharon?" Travis asked with a big grin on his face.

"Hmmm…she must be psychic!" Alison said, as she pulled her buzzing phone from her pocket, looking down to read the text that had just been delivered.

"Who's the text from?" Ty asked.

"It's not really any of your business." Alison curtly replied.

"I think I know…I bet it's from *Devon*."

"Stop it, Ty. He's just a friend." Ali said as she shot him 'the look'.

"It didn't look like he was just a friend, while you guys were decorating the gym. He was with you every second of the morning!"

"That's only because he wanted to talk to me about his new dog! He and his dad are both really excited because they get to pick him up this afternoon. The adoption is complete and he's really excited, and that's it, nothing more. Period. End of discussion." Alison informed her brother, as he looked at her with a smile on his face and a gleam in his eyes.

"Okay then, and again, where should we go for lunch?" Sharon interrupted the exchange between the siblings.

"Why don't we just get something to eat in the food court at the mall, if that's okay?" Ty asked.

"That sounds good to me, too." Alison added; glad that the subject had been changed from Devon, to Ty's favorite subject…food!

As they entered the mall's main entrance, the three momentarily stopped to gaze at the winter wonderland before them. Each year the decorations had become more elaborate, and this year, they seemed to have outdone themselves.

"This makes our gymnasium decorating look like nothing, compared to this place!" Ty said as he stood staring at the decorations that were hanging from the ceiling in the entrance.

"Well, what do you expect; we were on a very limited budget, compared to this place." Sharon added, as she stood looking up at the ceiling, also.

"Actually, I think our gym holds a close second to this place!" Ali added enthusiastically.

"You know what, Sis? I totally agree!"

"And I second that! This place doesn't have anything on us…after all; our place was decorated with a whole lot of love!" Sharon's statement punctuated everything that had just been said. "Now, off to the food court, before Ty faints from starvation!"

"Yes, feed me, please!" Ty added, as they all got onto the escalator that would take them right up to the food court.

At the top, Sharon, Ali and Ty all prepared to scatter in different directions, to check out their favorite fare. "Hey, guys, once you've decided what you want, let's meet at that table, the one that's right next to the Christmas tree that has the elf tree topper on it."

"Sounds like a plan." Ali said as she headed across the court towards the Chinese food, while her brother headed towards the pizza bar.

As the three of them sat together, eating the food that had appealed to their varied tastes, they discussed the different stores that they were all interested in visiting during the time that had been set aside to finish Christmas shopping.

"What do you need to get?" Alison asked, as she turned to look at her brother.

"Well, I need something for Mom…and for you."

"I just need something for Mom. Remember, we need to stick to something small and inexpensive, because Mom told us the same thing that she says every year…"

"Yah, 'kids, please don't get me anything, I already have everything I need'." Ty said, trying to mimic his mother's voice, causing both Sharon and Ali to break out into laughter.

"You sound just like her, Ty. That's the same thing she said to me when I walked into her classroom at school and asked her to give me some ideas. But, she's in luck, I had already pretty much decided on what I wanted to get her, so I'm just here, primarily, to spend time with the two of you!"

"Aw, thanks, Sharon. We really appreciate all the ways that you're always willing to help us out." Ali said as she scraped the last of her chow mein into a corner of the divider on her plate.

"I wonder how Mom's doing with Lucy. I bet she really misses us…Lucy, I mean, not Mom." Ty said as he prepared to finish off his pizza.

"I'm sure your mom misses both of you, too."

"Yah, I guess that you might be right. We've got a pretty good mom."

"Ty, we have the *best* of moms. So now, let's go find her some really special gifts, to let her know that she's appreciated." Alison rose from her seat, followed by Sharon and Ty, as they all headed to drop their trash into the can that was just across from the table where they sat.

All three of them began to hum along with some of the songs that were playing in the background, hopefully soothing some of the harried and hurried, even frantic, Christmas shoppers. The day was fast approaching and Sharon was glad that not only had she completed her Christmas shopping, but had also already shipped everything.

It didn't take long for both Ali and Ty to make their selections after visiting a small number of stores. With their bags in hand, the three decided to spend some extra time wandering the mall to enjoy the decorations and festivities that were going on around them.

"Hey, Ali," Ty said as he stood at the railing and looked down at the North Pole scene that had been set up on the floor below them, "Santa's here!"

"And?" Ali asked.

"Wanna go sit on his lap?" Ty mischievously asked.

"I think that your sister's a little old to sit on Santa's lap."

"I was only kidding. Actually, he just stepped behind the elf house and removed his jacket and the padding. Since he's fanning himself, he must be hot."

As Sharon looked over the railing to the scene below, she softly whistled. "That's not the old guy that usually comes here. The beard's fake."

"How do you know?" Ali asked as she joined Sharon and Ty, at the railing.

"Because he just pulled it down below his chin." Ty said, pointing down at him, using his thumb, so he could remain inconspicuous.

"And, you're exactly right, Ty! He *is* hot!" Sharon said, emphasizing the word 'hot'.

Ali began to laugh as she realized that Sharon wasn't talking about the man's temperature, rather, about the handsome face and the physique that had been well hidden under all of the padding. "I bet Sharon wouldn't mind sitting on a lap like that!" she added with a giggle.

"Hey, come on. Remember, I've sworn off men for the rest of my life! But there's never any harm in just looking, right Ali?"

"This conversation is my signal to move on." Ty said, as he turned to head back down the aisles of the mall.

"One of these days…" Sharon whispered to Ali, as they followed Ty, "he's going to realize that girls aren't something to be ignored."

"I agree, Sharon." Ali whispered back.

Chapter Twenty-eight

As the door opened, Travis looked into the incredible blue eyes of a very pretty, but disheveled woman, who appeared to be close to his own age. As he reached out towards her, offering to shake her hand and say hello, he couldn't help but wonder what she had been doing. The look on the young woman's face didn't seem to match the bold 'HO HO HO' statement on the front of her dirty sweatshirt. He could easily see that she had been crying, by the dirty swipe marks across both cheeks and her pony-tailed hair was sticking out all over the place.

"Good morning, ma'am. My name is Travis and I'm looking for Alison's mother. Is she here?"

"Yes, she is, and you're looking at her. May I ask what it is that you want?" Jamie asked with some trepidation, as she slowly reached out to shake the proffered hand. Too late, she had looked down and noticed her incredibly dirty hands and was amazed that someone so impeccably dressed hadn't missed a beat when he had taken the filthy hand in his own. "But I do have a name, and it's Jamie. To whom am I speaking?"

"My name is Travis and I'm hoping that we can discuss a matter that's very important to me."

Jamie hesitated, unsure if she should invite a total stranger into her home even though he had deeply dimpled cheeks and was tall, well dressed and extremely good looking. As she stood silently trying to decide whether to step outside or invite him in, Lucy peeked around the tree that had remained on the landing at the top of the stairs, yipped, and then ran down the stairs and straight to the stranger who was standing on her front porch.

As soon as Lucy got to Travis she began to wildly dance all around him, as if he was her new best friend. When Travis looked down and smiled at her, she went into overdrive in her dancing and barking and raised her paws up towards him, asking him to pick her up.

"Is it all right if I hold the dog?" He asked.

"Not a problem at all." Jamie replied as she watched Lucy jump and land safely in his arms as soon as he had bent down towards her. She began to whimper as she smothered his face with kisses and acted like he was someone she had previously known from her past.

"Oh, Lucy, I can't tell you how happy I am to see you! I thought we had lost you forever." Travis said as he gently stroked the happy little dog nestled snugly in his arms."

"Wait…how do you know Lucy?" Jamie asked, as she felt the sinking sensation of her stomach dropping to the floor.

"Actually, Lucy is the reason that I'm here. I know you've got to be feeling confused right now and it's a somewhat involved story. Is there somewhere that we could go to talk, where you'd feel safe, since I'm a complete stranger to you?"

"Obviously Lucy trusts you and since dogs seem to be pretty good character judges, would you like to come in? I'd rather not go anywhere dressed like this." Jamie said as she looked from her dirty hands to her dusty sweatshirt and the dirtied knees on her jeans. "I apologize, I must look like a real mess…I'm in the midst of a…project." Jamie said as she opened the door to allow the man to follow her indoors. "Come on upstairs, I just need to move the tree so we can get to the living room…or kitchen."

Travis continued to accept wet kisses from Lucy as he carried her, while following behind Jamie as she headed up the stairs. Once she had reached the landing, she grabbed the top of her bent over tree and began to drag it out of their path.

"So, I don't mean to presume, but it looks like you might have had a little problem with your tree?" Travis asked, attempting to keep from smiling as he looked upon the somewhat mangled mess that had previously been a six foot tall Christmas tree. "I've never seen one like this before. I've seen them upside down, but I've never seen one that appeared to be *bowing* to me."

Jamie couldn't help but notice the gleam in hazel colored eyes that were framed by incredibly thick eyelashes and his thick brown hair was perfectly combed, unlike Jamie's, as she suspected, was probably all over the place.

"Very funny! I'll have you know that this was once a beautiful tree. But the two of us tangled on the stairs and I clearly came out on top as the winner!"

As she and Travis both broke into laughter, Lucy joined in by punctuating their chuckles with some high pitched barking of her own.

"After I wash my hands, could I interest you in a cup of coffee?" Jamie asked.

"Coffee sounds great." Travis replied as Lucy began to rub her furry little head against his chin, while he followed Jamie into the small, but tidy, kitchen. As he watched her washing her hands at the sink, he wondered if he should mention that she might want to wash her face, also, but quickly decided against it. She actually looked quite cute with her messy hair and dirty face. Travis hoped that his decision to remain silent wouldn't cause any issues when she eventually realized that he hadn't spoken up.

As Jamie closed the door after Travis had left, she turned and caught a glimpse of her reflection in the mirror that hung on the wall of the entry way. With horror, she realized that she had sat and carried on a very serious conversation with Travis, while wearing, what she considered to be a scary and very dirty face; she wondered how he had managed to keep from breaking out into laughter while he was talking to her. *Oh well, so much for good, first impressions. It could have been worse…how, I'm not exactly sure. At least he was really kind…and good looking…oh my gosh! And I nonchalantly sat here, acting like there was nothing out of the normal going on! Hopefully he doesn't think that this is how I look all the time!*

Lucy sat at her feet and let out a soft whine. As Jamie bent to gather the little dog into her arms, her tears began to flow freely, coming from a wounded heart that was heavy with the knowledge that she had just learned during Travis's visit.

"Oh Lucy," Jamie sobbed, as she buried her face in the curly black fur. "How am I going to tell Ali and Ty that we have to send their little dog away? All because of a stupid will! No, it's not stupid. At least now I understand why you get so frantic whenever you hear a siren. And why you always seem to be looking for men."

Lucy let out another soft whine as she and Jamie headed up the stairs for the living room sofa, to sit together in front of the small, stone framed fireplace.

"You poor, precious little thing. To think that your beloved master left in an ambulance one day, never to return. It's no wonder that you get so afraid every time you hear a siren. It also makes me realize that you understand the grief that we've all been through. You've probably sensed our sadness as you were trying to deal with sadness of your own. Oh, Lucy, how are we going to face Christmas without you?" Jamie sobbed. "And how am I ever going to tell the kids that you'll be leaving…and…oh my goodness! I completely forgot about your collar…I forgot to tell Travis about your collar…oh well, it's not like I'm never going to see him again. After all, he'll be picking you up tomorrow evening. Lucy, how am I going to tell the kids?"

As if to answer, Lucy let out a long sigh as she lifted her head to look into Jamie's eyes, before letting out one final, soft whine, as she gently laid her head down on Jamie's lap.

Chapter Twenty-nine

As soon as Sharon's car pulled into the driveway, Lucy abandoned Jamie and bolted for the front door. As she sat waiting for the door to open, her little tail was wagging back and forth as fast as she could possible make it move.

As soon as the knob turned and the door opened, Lucy jumped up and animatedly began to bark a happy hello to the kids and Sharon as they came in through the door.

"Mom, we're home!" Ty yelled as he removed his snow dusted jacket. "And guess what? It's snowing again! I think that we're going to have a white Christmas this year!"

While Ali and Sharon removed their winter coats, Ty quickly headed up the stairs. When he found his mother sitting quietly on the sofa in the living room, he had a sinking feeling that something might be wrong.

"Are you okay, Mom?" he asked, as Ali came up the stairs carrying Lucy, with Sharon close behind.

When Jamie turned to look at all of them, it was easy to see that she had been crying.

"What's wrong, Mom?" Alison's concern was obvious on her face, and was being replicated by the look that Sharon wore.

Jamie patted the sofa beside her and tried to collect herself before she began to talk, "I have something to tell you kids."

"Should I leave?" Sharon asked.

"No, Sharon, I'd like for you to stay. You're family, and I'd like you here."

"What, Mom? What happened?" Ali asked, almost desperately.

"Everything's going to be okay," Jamie tried to reassure everyone, "and it's not the worst news, but it's not very happy news, either. A few hours ago, a man knocked on the door, because he had some information regarding Lucy."

Ali looked, somewhat desperately, into the face of the little dog that lay nestled in her arms. "What kind of information, Mom?"

"I don't even know how to tell you kids this. But, Lucy doesn't really belong to us and she's going to have to go to the home of her rightful owners."

"No…" Ali spoke, as she began to cry. "But they gave her up. And now, have they decided that they want to have her back?"

Sharon and Ty both sat silently, listening to everything that Jamie had begun to tell all of them.

"It's complicated, Ali. The people who surrendered Lucy weren't supposed to. She didn't belong to them, so they really had no right to surrender her to the shelter."

"Had they just found her somewhere, and decided to take her to the pound?" Ty asked.

"No, they hadn't found her. Lucy belonged to an elderly man named John. Unfortunately, he had a heart attack, so his adult kids had taken custody of her. When neither of them wanted to keep Lucy, they decided to surrender her to the shelter."

"I still don't understand, Mom. Do they want her back?" Ali spoke again, while hugging Lucy tightly to her.

"No, Ali. As I said, it's complicated. The man who owned Lucy was wealthy, and he had a will. Lucy was going to be provided for, according to his will, and he had left Lucy to one of his best friends. So, Lucy should have never been given up. His kids didn't have that right."

"So, it's almost like, if someone found a dog and then gave it away to the pound without notifying the owner? So, it wasn't their dog to give away?" Ty asked.

"That's almost exactly how it is, Ty."

"But, Jamie, this seems so unfair! There's got to be something that you can do, so that you and the kids can keep her."

"Oh, Sharon, I've gone over and over this in my mind and I feel like we need to do what's right. Giving Lucy to the people that her owner intended her to live with is the right thing to do."

"No, Mom…" Ali's voice trailed off as she turned to bury her face in one of the pillows on the sofa.

"Ali, it's not going to be goodbye forever when Lucy leaves here. The lawyer representing Lucy told me that his parents are the ones who will be keeping her. He said that he's going to make sure that we all get visitation rights."

"So in other words, it's almost like a child custody case?" Sharon asked. "Lucy will go back and forth like the children of divorced parents? Unbelievable!"

"This started out as what was going to be a wonderful Christmas! And now, everything's all messed up. Christmas is messed up again." Ty's sadness was easily seen on his face, as he continued to hold back the tears.

"I'm so sorry, kids. I don't know if it will help much, but Lucy knows the people who will be keeping her, so she should be really happy while she's living with them."

As Ali lifted her head out of the pillow, she asked, "When will Lucy be leaving us, Mom?"

"He's going to pick her up tomorrow afternoon. Believe me, Ali, he feels as bad about all of this as we do. But, he has to honor his client's wishes."

"How was he even able to locate Lucy?" Sharon asked.

"He took the limited information that he had and started looking into what might have happened to her. Thankfully, the Misfit Rescue had picked her up, so that she hadn't been destroyed. He eventually located Susan and met with her."

"Why didn't Susan tell us?" Alison asked.

"Because she just found out a few days ago, herself. The man, Travis, had asked her not to say anything until after he met with us. Since you were all out for the day, he told me everything that had happened, so that I could break the news to you. So, please, don't be angry at Susan, Ali."

"I'm not, Mom. I won't be. It's not her fault…may I be excused to go to my room with Lucy?"

"Yes, you may. I'm so sorry, Ali and Ty. As your mom, I just wish that I could make this better."

"I do too, Mom, but there are a lot of things in life that a mom just can't make better." Ty said softly, as he rose to his feet to follow Alison up the stairs to their rooms.

As Jamie and Sharon sat commiserating side by side on the couch, neither of them had much of anything to say.

"On a bright side," Sharon finally spoke, "at least you're all going to get to see Lucy. That's something to be grateful for."

"I know, Sharon. I've been telling myself that ever since Travis came by to 'drop the bomb'."

"Did I tell you that there was a new Santa at the mall today?"

"No. Other than the crisis surrounding Lucy, I don't know anything about how today went. A new Santa, huh?"

"Yah, and he wasn't an old guy, he was young, and very good looking, not to mention really buff! Wanna see if you can sit on his lap and tell him that all you want for Christmas is a little black dog that belongs to someone else?" Sharon asked, attempting to lighten their moods.

"Good looking and buff, huh? Not interested and I doubt that he can make any of my Christmas wishes come true. I wonder how the little kids reacted to him. Even they had to know that the guy was a fake." Jamie finally smiled.

"With the fake beard and all of the padding, he must have done okay, because the lines of kids snaked all over the North Pole."

"Sometimes I wish that my kids were still small enough to want to go and visit Santa. They're growing up so fast that one of these days, before I know it, they'll both be leaving me behind and heading off to college."

"When that day comes, my friend, you'll still have me. And I'm not sure if that's a good thing or a bad thing!" Sharon cracked another smile.

Jamie finally chuckled, "That has and will always be, a very good thing!"

"Since you finally look like you're going to be okay, I should probably be heading home to Tigger. I'm sure that by now he's either shredded a pair of my panty hose or he's knocked most of the decorations off my tree…speaking of trees, what on earth happened to yours? It looks like it's been in a war zone."

"You don't even want to know…and the way it looks now is good compared to what it looked like before Travis straightened it right before he left. We were supposed to decorate it tonight. It doesn't look like that's going to happen. You know, Sharon, Travis *is* a really nice guy. He feels awful about what's happened. He seems to be a kind and caring person and he's good looking, besides."

"Good looking? I didn't think that you even noticed anything like that when it came to men." Sharon wore a look of surprise, as she looked in Jamie's direction.

"I might be a widow, Sharon, but I do have a great set of eyes that see everything quite clearly, thanks to 20/20 vision."

"And on that note, I'll take my leave so that I can head home to my furry friend." Sharon said as she rose to give her friend a hug goodbye.

Chapter Thirty

"Well, Lucy," Travis said, as he put his car in drive to pull away from the home of the heart broken family he had just left behind. "I feel like a complete schmuck."

Once he'd traveled a few blocks from Jamie's condo, Travis pulled off to the side of the road and stopped. *All because of written words on paper; all because of a will that I'm obligated to fulfill.* For the first time in his years as a lawyer, he wished that he could go and destroy the will and return Lucy to the family that she had already found.

Alison had quickly fled the room as soon as she'd realized that her little dog was really going to be leaving her. Ty had held it together, Travis suspected, attempting to be the man of the family. Jamie had also stood stoically by as they had surrendered their beloved little pet. *If only Dad hadn't promised John that he and Mom would give Lucy a home if anything ever happened to him…if only…*

He thought again of Jamie, this time, her beautiful hair had been neatly pulled back into a French braid and the muddy streaks across her face had been completely eradicated. He smiled as he recalled her reprimand about his negligence to say anything about her disheveled state, when he had stopped by on the previous morning.

"Mr. Redman, I have a bone to pick with you!" she'd said as soon as he had been received into her home again, after being introduced to her children.

He'd 'pleaded the fifth' with his arms in the air, as he'd apologized for having kept his silence the day before, while she had invited him in, completely unaware of the fact that she looked like she had just slathered mud onto her cheeks. Travis had, once again, noticed her beautiful blue eyes, as they seemed to smile with the laughter that they'd shared regarding their initial meeting.

When he looked over at Lucy, who had settled herself onto the bucket seat beside him, she had lay down and placed her head onto the scarf that she held comfortingly between her paws.

"You're sad, too, aren't you, Lucy?" he asked.

As she picked up her head and turned to look at him, he noticed what looked like tears in both of her little brown eyes.

"Yes, you are, little girl. You're not much different than we humans. You feel happiness and sadness, and you even grieve like us, don't you?" He said as he reached over to gently scratch the top of her head. "I do have a little surprise for you, girl. You're going to get to meet one of your ex-housemates…its Rascal…I hope that you guys will be happy to see each other. You'll also get to meet your new owners. I know that you'll remember them and I think you'll be happy when you go to live with them. They're really looking forward to seeing you again and I think that you're going to end up being almost as spoiled as you used to be."

Lucy let out a whine that sounded just like she was asking "Huh?" Then, stood onto her hind legs and began to look out the window, as if searching for someone.

"I bet you still miss John, don't you little girl?"

Lucy yipped as soon as she'd heard the word "John" and then cocked her head sideways before excitedly turning to resume gazing at the scenery through the car's window. She began to softly whine and then to pant excitedly, as Travis put the car into drive and headed towards home.

As he turned the steering wheel and began to merge into oncoming traffic, the diamond collar that he had slipped onto his wrist caught his eye. It had been obvious to him that Jamie and her family could have benefitted from selling the collar and pocketing the money. He'd almost wished that they had. He'd often felt like the collar had been a dangerous extravagance to have on the neck of a little dog, owned by an elderly man. *John, you could have been mugged and little Lucy stolen, just for this expensive collar…but I'm sure, just as Jamie had thought it was rhinestones or zirconia, everyone who ever came into contact probably thought the same. Thank goodness!*

"Well, Lucy, I think that we'll probably sell your diamond 'choker' and provide the family with a little Christmas reward for taking such good care of you, don't you think?"

Lucy turned from looking out the window to give a little yip in Travis's direction.

"And if they won't take it, which I assume they probably won't, then we'll donate the money to the Misfit Rescue. Susan, I'm sure, can put the money to very good use. And for the rest of your inheritance, since my folks won't take any of it, maybe we can set up a 'Lucy Trust' that can be there for not only the Misfits, but for other animal rescues, also."

Lucy began to excitedly yip at Travis and came over to give his hand a quick lick, before settling herself back onto her seat to stare straight ahead, at the glove compartment before her.

"Gosh, Lucy…I'm always amazed at how much human language dogs seem to understand. I feel bad that we humans can't seem to figure out what it is you guys are trying to say to us. But, I'll take your yips as an affirmative response to my plans for your estate!" Travis said as he pulled into the driveway of his home.

He looked at the living room window as he waited for the door to open, looking to see if there was a little blonde, furry face peering out the window. He'd already come to cherish the fact that Rascal watched him back out of the drive each time he had to leave the house and that he was always there, patiently waiting by the door when he had returned. Even though he'd only had him for a few days, he was enjoying the relationship that they were slowly beginning to build. He had to chuckle when he thought about the way that Rascal let him know whenever he disapproved of anything. He'd simply turn his back on him and sit silently, until Travis finally went away.

"Come on Lucy, it's time to go in and say hello to Dad and Mom. I know that they're going to be really happy to see you…I hope you'll feel the same way, once you recognize them. And don't worry. We'll be seeing Ali and her family on Christmas Day; after all, they *will* get very generous visitation rights, it's already been arranged."

Travis said as he opened the passenger door and lifted Lucy off the seat to carry her into the house.

"Here she is." Travis said as he walked through the door, immediately noticing that Rascal was sitting with his back to his parents, where they sat together on the couch. As soon as he set Lucy down onto the floor, she began to jump around and frantically begin her high pitched barking. As Lucy continued to bark, Rascal soon turned around to look to see what was going on, immediately recognizing Lucy, he began to run toward his little black friend.

For the first time, Travis and his parents had an opportunity to see Rascal come to life as he hopped like a bunny, running towards Lucy. She couldn't seem to decide where to go first, so she quickly ran to Rascal, gave him a quick sniff and a kiss and then ran to greet Travis's parents by jumping onto first one lap and then, the other. Rascal continued to show his excitement by running around the room like a mad man. As he ran from the living room into the tiled entry way, his feet slid on the slick floor and sent him sliding on his side, into the kitchen. After getting back onto his feet, he ran back to the living room, hopping onto the sofa to sit next to Lucy who was rubbing her head all over Mary's arm.

"Oh my goodness," she said as she petted both Lucy and Rascal. "Travis, we really thought that Rascal had no personality, but he's definitely proving us wrong!"

"I know, Mom, I've never seen him this animated! I didn't think he had so much life in him! This is wonderful to see that there's a playful side to him." Travis said, as Rascal jumped down off the sofa to run to Travis to be petted, and then back to the sofa, to sit next to David. "Lucy seems to remember both of us; I had been a little worried that she might not."

"I don't think that dogs ever forget," Mary said as she took Lucy back onto her lap, "remember how B.J. never forgot Travis, after he went away to college."

As Lucy and Rascal both jumped down onto the floor, they began to chase one another around the room. Each time Lucy barked, Rascal responded by running in her direction.

"I don't think that Rascal is totally deaf, Travis. He seems to be able to hear Lucy when she barks."

"I don't think there's anyone who can't hear Lucy's shrill bark, Dad. I'm pretty sure that she'd be able to wake the dead!"

Chapter Thirty-one

"Is anyone interested in decorating the tree tonight?" Jamie asked as she and the kids began to clear the dinner table.

"I'm game." Ty said as he carried his dishes to the sink. "How about you, Ali?"

"I don't feel much like it, but I'll help anyway." She said, with a sigh. "I just wish that Lucy was going to be here to watch us."

"I'm so sorry, Ali. I really wish that things had turned out differently. One of these days we can get another dog."

"I don't think I want another dog, Mom. I just wanted Lucy or Rascal and he's gone, too. I'm not sure that I want to give my heart to another pet…at least not for a while anyway."

"That goes for me, too." Ty added, as he began to rifle through the junk drawer. "I'll get the box cutter and open the boxes of decorations."

"Thanks, Ty. We'll finish up here in a minute and we can get started after that. Ali, would you want to switch on some Christmas music? Maybe that will help us to get into a slightly more festive mood."

"K" Ali answered, as she dried her hands on the kitchen towel and went to choose a channel on the radio.

As they started taking ornaments out of the boxes, their moods began to lift slightly as they laughed over some of the ones that had been made when they kids were much younger.

"Look at this one! Do you remember when I gave it to you, Mom? I was so proud of this clay creation. And you had no idea what on earth it was!"

"I did too; I recognized right away that it was an angel!"

"Only after I told you that it was an angel!" Alison laughed while she turned the ornament around. "See, here's the head, and these were supposed to be the wings."

"Is that what those things are?" Jamie asked, happy to see her daughter's smile.

"I think mine is even worse than yours, Sis." Ty said as he held up a round ornament that was supposed to be a snowman's head. "It looks like something out of a horror movie, don't you think? Mom, why don't you throw these things away?"

"I save them for the memories that they bring back. Memories of when you were small, and your hideous ornaments had been lovingly presented to me as gifts on Christmas morning."

"Oh great, I keep hoping that you'll eventually replace some of our pre-school ornaments with something a little nicer! In fact, one day, I'd love to decorate our tree with just glittery bows and white lights. We could have a glam tree, something really feminine and chic. Something to make people ooh and aah over." Ali said, as she continued to hang ornaments on the tree.

"Oh no, no way do I ever want to have a chic, glam, *girly* tree! That's definitely nothing that a guy would ever be interested in having around! I'll take the ugly pre-school ornaments over that, any day!"

"You don't have to worry about it this year, son. We're sticking with our old, traditional, handmade ornaments."

"But, Mom, would you be willing to make a deal with Ty and me?"

"That depends on what kind of a deal it is." Jamie looked at her daughter with a perplexed look on her face.

"Well, Ty and I had discussed this last Christmas, while we were taking the ornaments off the tree."

"We did? Discussed what?" Now it was Ty with a perplexed look on his face.

"Remember, we said that we were going to talk to Mom about replacing some of our old, ugly ornaments, slowly and one at a time. Then, after Christmas, during the sales, we wanted to purchase one new Hallmark ornament to replace one that we wanted to do away with."

"Oh, now I remember. That way we could exchange one ornament for another and slowly get rid of some of those 'what on earth is it?' ornaments! So, Mom, would you at least think about it?"

"Who would decide which ornaments would be the ones to go?" Jamie asked. "Will I have any say in it?"

"No!" both kids responded together.

"We'll each pick just one ornament after Christmas is over; some of the embarrassing ones, like that angel, and we'll get a nice one to hang in its place. Ty and I can give them a proper send off, right into the trash can!"

"Yes, Mom, we'll give them a *proper* send off, to go where no ornament has ever gone before!" Ty said, as they all broke out into laughter.

"That way, one day in the future, our tree won't look so much like it belongs at a homeless shelter!" Ali added.

"Okay, we'll give it a try, but I can't promise you that I'll be able to fully approve every one of your choices. I'll get to be 'Judge Mom'. I'll want to be the one who can *pardon* some of the ornaments if I just can't bear to part with them."

As Alison and Ty both turned to look at each other, they reached their hands out to Jamie, so that they could all shake on it.

"Deal." Ty said as he shook his mother's hand.

"Same here." Ali responded to her brother's comment, while shaking hands.

After they had finished hanging the last of the ornaments, Ty carried the boxes down the stairs, to return them to their place in the crawl space.

"Hey! Look outside! It's snowing!" he said as he came back into the house.

Both Jamie and Alison went to look out the living room window and saw that a gentle snow had begun to fall, softly covering everything in a blanket of white.

"Since it's only eight o'clock, how would you kids like to go for a ride to look at Christmas lights?"

"Yes!" Ty answered.

"What about Sharon, she usually goes along with us."

"Would you call her, Ali? I'm going to start making some hot chocolate to take along with us."

"And don't forget the candy canes, Mom."

"I've got another box of them in the pantry, Ty, would you grab them for me, please? We definitely don't want them to be left behind…after all…"

"It's tradition." Ty finished his mother's sentence with a grin.

Sharon paused her Christmas movie after hearing the phone ring and ran to find it, calling to her from somewhere inside her closet. *Who on earth would be calling me at this time on a school night?*

"Hello?"

"Hi Sharon, this is Ali."

"I saw that when I finally found my phone. Is everything okay?"

"Yep, everything is fine. So, Sharon…what are you wearing?"

"Ali…what…is this a trick question?"

"Nope. I'm just curious."

"Well, I'm wearing my pajamas. It's the perfect apparel for the Christmas movie that I *was* watching.

"Perfect! We're going to pick you up in fifteen minutes, so leave your pajamas on because that's what we're all wearing, too. Well, except Mom, she's in a Christmas-y pair of sweats; she figured one of us needed to have something substantial on, just in case we were to get stuck in the snow. Speaking of which, be sure to wear your winter boots…it's snowing!"

"O…kay…can I ask where we're going in our pajamas?"

"Oh yah, I almost forgot to tell you…we're going to drive around and look at Christmas lights while we drink hot cocoa. Since we didn't get around to it last year, we *have* to go this year! After all…"

"It's tradition!" Sharon finished her sentence. "I'll be waiting."

"Perfect. We'll be over to get you in fifteen minutes." Ali said as she hung up the phone.

Chapter Thirty-two

As Ty came tramping down the stairs from his room, Jamie looked at him and smiled. He looked so tall and handsome in a white shirt and red tie, topped with a light gray sweater. His black cuffed pants made his legs look even longer than they usually did. He was the epitome of classiness in his mother's eyes…except for the pair of sneakers that he wore on his feet.

"Ty, where are your dress shoes?"

"Mom, they hurt my feet! And besides, who cares what I have on my feet? It's not like I'm going to the dance to impress anyone. Unlike Ali, who I'm sure, is dressing to impress *De…von.*"

"Would you please just drop it, Ty?" Alison asked as she descended the stairs wearing a fitted ivory top together with a pleated burgundy skirt over a pair of black tights. She had added a black velvet double breasted jacket and had finished everything off with a pair of black velvet knee boots.

"Wow, Sis, you look really nice for a change."

"I agree with you, Ty, but you could have left off the 'for a change' part of your comment."

"You guys are going to make me blush, so just hush, please." Ali said as she entered the living room to take her place in front of the fireplace for pictures. She and Ty knew that their mom was going to insist on taking a bunch of them before she'd allow any of them to walk out the door.

Jamie, also, was nicely dressed. She, like Ali, had chosen a black blazer to top the red fitted dress that she was wearing. Instead of black tights, she wore panty hose with a pair of black boots. She and Sharon were some of the adults who had volunteered to chaperone during the school dance again this year.

"You look nice, too, Mom." Ty said as he took her phone from her and began taking selfies of them, together, in front of the fireplace.

"Thank you, Ty. Flattery will get you everywhere, so, with that very kind statement, I guess I'll allow you to wear your tennis shoes to the dance."

"Yes!" Ty said as he handed back the phone and pumped the air with his fist and headed down the stairs, for the garage.

"Are you ready to go, Ali?" Jamie asked, once again admiring what a beautiful young woman her daughter was rapidly becoming.

"I am; I just need to grab my purse. I think I left it in my room, so I'll head out in just a minute."

"Okay, we'll be waiting for you in the car."

When they arrived at the school auditorium, the three immediately noticed Sharon waving to them from one of the tables that was nearest the front of the room. With her usual eclectic style, Sharon's outfit was interesting, to say the least. She, like Jamie, was in a red dress. The skirt of hers' flared out over a pair of horizontally striped green and white leggings. Unlike Jamie, she had topped her dress with a bright green velvet jacket, the bottom fringed with tiny gold bells, sporting a black patent leather belt, with a large gold buckle. She had finished it off with a pair of Doc Marten black boots, with buckles on the sides of them. Jamie no longer had any reservations about the shoes that Ty had chosen to wear!

"Well, well, well," Sharon said as Jamie and the kids approached the table where she was standing, "don't you all look nice!"

"Thank you." Jamie replied first, then Ali.

"Aw, shucks." Ty said as he looked down towards the floor, appearing to be shy.

"Oh stop with the act, Ty" Sharon added with a laugh. "Now, I have some jobs to delegate, if you're all willing to lend a hand."

"Definitely; what would you like us to do?" Jamie asked.

"Jamie, if you'll pour the sodas and juice into the punch bowls that have been set up on these two tables, I'll go to the teacher's lounge and get the sherbet."

"Ty and Ali, if you'll follow me to the lounge, I'll need you to begin carrying the cookies and cakes to set up onto all the rest of the tables. And Ty?"

"Yes?" he momentarily stopped to listen.

"Even though I'm sure that you're more than likely starving," Sharon pointedly looked his direction, "you can't start eating the goodies until the rest of the students begin to arrive!"

"Me? Eat the goodies before I'm supposed to? You *must* be thinking of some other goodie stealing thief…everything is definitely safe with me!"

"Yah, right." Alison added, while Sharon stood behind her shaking her head affirmatively.

It didn't take long before the punch bowls had been filled, topped with generous scoops of multi-colored sherbet while the rest of the tables had been covered with all of the goodies that had been provided by parent volunteers.

As Jamie and Sharon perused the tables that were holding the plates of cookies, bars and cupcakes, they were amazed at all the creativity some of the parents had put into their desserts.

"Some of these women must have entirely too much time on their hands, or at least more time on their hands than I do!" Sharon said as she looked at some of the intricate decorating details. "Some of this looks too nice to even eat!"

"I'm amazed at the abilities of some of the bakers! I *wish* that I could duplicate some of their ideas! I mean, look at these gingerbread men. They're beautiful! Ours always look like the gingerbread men who weren't able to run away!"

"Huh?" Sharon asked.

"You know; the old nursery rhyme!" Jamie replied.

"Oh yah, now I do. 'Run, run, as fast as you can, you can't catch me, I'm the gingerbread man'."

"Yes, ours look like the ones who couldn't get away and they must have been thrown around!"

Both Sharon and Jamie broke into laughter, as they were joined by some of the other chaperones.

"Can you believe some of these desserts?" one of the women asked, wide eyed. "I wish I had the ability to make my cookies look this good!"

At that, Sharon added, "We were just saying the same, exact thing! And, oh, look, I think that we're about to get this show on the road! I think the D.J. has just arrived!"

As Jamie, Sharon and the other volunteers worked to make sure that the tables remained well stocked; the kids had all begun to gather into different groups that lined the walls of the room. A few of the older boys and girls had finally gotten up the courage to head out on the floor to dance. The D.J. had a play list of the most popular tunes that appealed to the teens. He had also generously sprinkled in a Christmas song here and there. Whenever the Christmas songs were played, the kids usually made a long chain and snaked their way around the room, while singing along with the music.

Sharon had been up to her usual behavior throughout the dance. Since she had such a heart for the kids with special needs, she was seen dancing with a variety of the students from the special education program. Some of them, in wheelchairs, were wheeled around in circles by their very exuberant dance partner. Others were learning a variety of steps, based on their abilities. Once Sharon had gotten them out onto the dance floor, she took it upon herself to encourage the other students to step into her place, who had continued to make sure that all of the kids felt included.

"Whew! I need a break! I'm getting too old for all of this!" Sharon said as she poured herself a cup of punch and grabbed one of the brownie cupcakes that had been decorated to look like a reindeers' face, wearing pretzels as antlers.

"Sharon, you'll never be too old for any of this!" Jamie laughed. "In fact, I can imagine you out on the dance floor with your cane in hand!"

"Oh, Jamie, have you noticed that Ali and Devon have been together almost the entire evening?"

"Yes, I have, but I've been keeping my distance. I don't want Ali to feel self-conscious about having her mother here at the dance. But, on another note, have you noticed Ty tonight?"

"You'd better believe I have! That's a really adorable little gal that he's been talking to, don't you think?"

"Oh yes. They both seemed a little shy around one another at first, but you could have knocked me over with a feather when I saw him take her hand to lead her over to the chain dance, during 'Jingle Bell Rock'!"

"I know! I was part of that chain, just a few people behind them! I wanted to keep my distance so he wouldn't bolt for the door!"

"I'm just afraid that it's happening, Sharon."

"What's happening?"

"The fact that Ty has reached the age where…"

"Girls no longer have cooties!" Sharon finished Jamie's sentence for her. "Oh, do you hear that? The D.J. is going to finish up the dance with the song 'Hokey Pokey'! Come on, Jamie, you have to dance this one! After all…"

"It's tradition!" Jamie laughed as she finished Sharon's sentence and headed out onto the dance floor with her friend.

Chapter Thirty-three

As Ty walked sleepily into the kitchen, he yawned and stretched before asking, "What's for breakfast, Mom?"

"I thought that I'd make us all some French toast once your sister gets up. Does that sound okay?" Jamie asked, before taking another sip of her coffee.

"Sounds great, Mom." Ty shuffled into the living room to turn on the television. "No rush, Ali's still sleeping and I'm not that hungry after all the stuff I ate last night."

"You, not that hungry? Are you okay?" Jamie asked with concern.

As Ty felt of his forehead, he looked over to reassure her, "No fever. I must be fine. Maybe I'm not growing as fast as I was. Either that or my stomach's on a break, like the rest of me. But don't worry, Mom. By the time you make breakfast, I'll be hungry, I promise!"

As he turned up the volume on the television, Jamie finished off her coffee and rose from her stool at the breakfast bar to begin gathering the ingredients that she'd need to make the French toast.

She had no sooner finished frying up some bacon, when Ali walked into the kitchen to pour herself half a cup of milk with two spoons of sugar. She finished filling it with coffee, before setting it in the microwave to warm it up.

"Smells good, Mom," she said as she took her drink with her, to sit on one of the stools at the bar. "It looks like we're having

French toast, too. Yum, it's been awhile since we've had time for something other than a quick bowl of cereal."

"I agree, Ali. I'm so glad that we all have this break from school. December has been a rough and busy month. I think we all really need the time off."

"Are we doing anything today?"

"Nothing planned. I figured that this could be a lazy day, since we were out pretty late after cleaning up at the dance last night. I thought it might be nice to veg in front of the television to watch some of the Christmas movie marathons. And tomorrow, I thought that we could do some Christmas baking."

"That sounds perfect, to me." Ali added, as she finished off her drink. "I've got a new Christmas book that I wanted to start on. I'm hoping I can finish it off by Christmas Eve, on Sunday."

"That's only three days away."

"I know, but it's a short novel about a rescue dog, so three days is more than enough time to polish it off. And, speaking of the rescues, Susan gave me the day off, today. Tomorrow and Saturday I'll need to go in for a couple of hours to help with their care, while Susan is out finishing things for herself for Christmas."

"I definitely won't be doing any reading at all for the next couple of weeks." Ty said, cupping his hands around his mouth, from his perch on the living room sofa. "I'm on break and so are my eyes and my brain! They're on break right along with me!"

"I don't feel much different than you do, Son. I'm going to do as much 'nothing' as I can cram into this holiday season! Now, everything's ready, so come and eat."

"Oh good, because…"

"He's starving." Ali finished her brother's sentence with a laugh as she carried the syrup and juice to the table.

"Mom…Sharon's here to bake cookies with us!" Ty yelled up the stairs from the entryway, after opening the door.

"Come on up, Sharon." Jamie said as she walked to the top of the stairs to welcome her friend for the day's activities.

"Can I get you something to drink?" Ali asked as Sharon entered the kitchen, carrying a bag of ingredients.

"Sure, what are you drinking?"

"Peppermint hot chocolate, want some?"

"That sounds good, but do you mind adding some coffee crystals to mine? I do that all the time at home and it makes me feel like I'm drinking Café Mocha."

"Do we have any crystals, Mom?" Ali asked.

"We do. If you look in the cupboard where I keep the cocoa, you should find a small jar tucked in the back of the cabinet. So, are you ready for Christmas?" Jamie asked as she turned to look at Sharon, who had begun unloading her bag.

"After today I will be." She replied, setting bags of white and dark chocolate chips down onto the breakfast bar. "I also found a big bag of almonds for the bark. Were you able to locate the raw peanuts for the peanut brittle?"

"Finally, after I had to run to three different stores yesterday afternoon, in between movies. I can't believe that I forgot to buy them a few weeks back. Some ingredients are hard to find if you wait too long to purchase them. In fact, I won't be making any of my Grandma's fruitcake this year; I haven't been able to find any of the candied fruits."

"Yuck! I hate fruitcake!" Ty yelled down from his bedroom at the top of the stairs.

"We know you do! It's only because you refuse to try my Grandma's recipe!" Jamie hollered back at her son.

"Mom! I'd get in trouble for yelling up the stairs at my brother like you just did."

"I know, double standards. But sometimes, I get to use my 'Mom' card in order to get out of jail free."

"You *are* right, Mom. Ty has no idea what he's missing when it comes to Grandma's recipe. Remember the first time I ever tried it?"

"How could I forget? You had your dad cut you a microscopic piece of it that I was just sure you'd end up spitting into the sink, and you surprised us when you asked for more."

"It's Grandma's secret ingredients…chocolate chips and macadamia nuts make *everything* taste better."

"Oh, yum! Can we quit talking about baking and actually start mixing and baking instead?" Sharon said, as she used her hand to make a circular motion over the center of her stomach.

"Now you look just like Ty!" Jamie said as she began to crack eggs into the metal mixing bowl that she had set out on the countertop.

As Ali arranged a variety of their freshly baked cookies, almond bark and fudge onto a plate, Ty was busy putting another bag of popcorn into the microwave. They had finished all the baking late in the afternoon. Jamie had been glad that she'd had a container of chili in the freezer that she had thawed and heated to help everyone balance all the sugar that they had ingested while doing the cooking. The consensus had been to finish off the evening with popcorn, goodies and a movie.

"And after we're done watching 'A Christmas Story', I'll be ready to head home to Tigger," Sharon said, as she yawned, "get into my jammies and crawl in bed to finish my Christmas novel."

"Me, too, Sharon. I'm reading a Christmas book about some rescue dogs and it's been so good that I'll probably be finishing it up tonight when I go to bed to read."

"Not me." Ty added to the conversation. "I'm staying away from books for the next two weeks!"

"But Ty, reading for enjoyment is a lot different than reading to learn something for school."

"I've told him the same thing about a hundred times, Sharon. I've also told him that a person is able to go *anywhere* in a book. Exotic places, scary places, some place where a person has never been before."

"Nah, not for me. I'm happy being right here in my own home. I don't need a book to go anywhere. I can go to all those places when I watch t.v., too, you know."

"Mom, he does have a point. But everyone in this family has always loved to read! There's got to be something seriously wrong with him…either that, or he's adopted. Yep, that must be the problem. Ty, I think that you're adopted!" Ali said as she gently popped her brother in his side with her closed fist.

“Mom…Ali’s being mean to me. She told me I’m adopted.” Ty said with an exaggerated whine.

“Ali, be nice to your brother.” Jamie said as she smiled, while pushing ‘play’ on the remote.

Chapter Thirty-four

As Jamie began dressing for the Christmas Eve candlelight services, she heard the sound of Alison's hair dryer, as she was getting ready in the bathroom. Ty lightly knocked, before poking his head in the door to Jamie's room.

"I'm wearing the same thing that I wore to the dance, Mom. And I even managed to squeeze my feet into my dress shoes."

"Are your poor feet going to be okay?"

"Yah, they'll live. It's only for a couple of hours and this time, I won't be dancing."

"Speaking of dancing…I've been meaning to ask you who the blonde girl was, that I saw you talking with at the dance."

"Aw, she's nobody. Her name is Samantha. We call her Sam. She's just a friend from school; but she *is* really pretty, don't you think? I mean, for a girl, that is."

"Yes, very pretty, Ty. Is she nice?"

"She's really nice. She's so kind to everyone, even to the boys! But there's just one thing, Mom?"

"What's that?"

"Please don't ever tell Ali that I said that I think she's pretty. I'd *never* be able to live it down!"

"Your secret is safe with me, Ty." Jamie said, as she stepped toward her son to tenderly straighten a few of the wild hairs near the part in his hair. When she had finished, Ty surprised her by wrapping his arms around her, to give her a hug. "But just remember, she probably doesn't feel any differently about things whenever you refer to Devon."

"Is it okay if I have a few more cookies before we leave?" he asked.

"Yes, sir, you may. After all, I wouldn't want you to be starving by the time we get to church!"

Moments after Alison's hair dryer shut off, she emerged from the bathroom, dressed and ready for church.

"You look nice." Jamie said, noting that Alison was in the same skirt that she had worn to the dance, but she had topped it with a white sweater that had two small black reindeer woven into the pattern. She had also changed to white tights to go with a pair of chunky heeled white boots.

"Thanks, Mom. So do you."

"We should probably get going so we can get Sharon picked up and get to the church before it's too crowded. Ty's having a few cookies before we leave. Are you hungry?"

"No, I'm still full from the snacks that I ate before I got in the shower. And I know that we'll be eating again, once we get home."

"I'll be down as soon as I finish touching up my make-up. Will you let your brother know that we'll be leaving in just a few minutes? And will you also make sure that he's not eating every cookie that we own?" Jamie asked as she watched her daughter descending the stairs.

When Jamie, Sharon and the kids entered the church, it was already beginning to fill up. They ended up finding seating toward the back, but they still had a good view of everything that would soon be taking place. An elevated stage held the risers that the choir members would be standing on, while performing some of the most popular Christmas carols, between the readings of the Christmas story.

Each year, the church's choir formed a 'human' Christmas tree because of the way the risers were set in place. The lowest riser was the widest, with each one getting shorter in length as they graduated upwards. With the choir's dark green robes and each member wearing alternating red and white bows, it gave the appearance of being a tree that had been decked out with Christmas bows. A single member, usually a soloist, stood on the top riser, wearing a gold star headgear that helped to complete the illusion.

As the church continued to fill, the musicians sitting in the semi-circle of chairs in front of the stage began to softly play. As the lights dimmed, the electric candles that lined the edge of the stage, together with the luminaries that lined the rows of pews, promoted a strong sense of serene peacefulness. As Jamie looked over at Ty and Alison, sitting next to her, she noted the somber looks on each of their faces. She couldn't help but wonder if they, like her, were remembering Christmas's past. Christmas's when they were still a family of four.

She eventually noticed Ty beginning to smile, nudge Ali and then lean over to whisper something in her ear. When Ali smiled back at him, she shook her head in affirmative acknowledgement, as her shoulders began to shake from the laughter she was holding inside. When Jamie tapped Ty, her furrowed brow seemed to ask him what he had told his sister that was so funny. He silently held one finger up, as his own shoulders began to shake from silent laughter. When he finally got himself in check, he leaned towards Jamie, so that he could tell her what was going on.

"I was reminding Ali of the year, back when they gave everyone real candles, that I accidentally lit her bangs on fire!" He softly whispered in his mother's ear.

It didn't take long for Jamie to join in on the silent laughter, as she noticed Sharon looking at all of them like they had just lost their minds.

"I promise, Sharon, I'll tell you all about this on the way home." Jamie whispered.

"You'd better!" Sharon whispered back, as the curtain in front of the stage slid back to reveal the choir, as they began singing 'Oh Holy Night'.

After they had finished greeting other church members, and sharing many hugs and 'Merry Christmas's', they finally made their way to the SUV, to begin the drive home. While they had all been inside the church, the snow had once again begun to fall, covering everything with a white blanket that looked like diamonds, every time the light reflected off the snow.

"Oh, this is so beautiful!" Sharon said as they began to slowly move along. "Now, let's cut to the chase…what was it that you were all whispering about that was so funny, while we were sitting in church?"

"You tell it, Ty. After all, you were the culprit that caused the whole debacle!" Jamie said, as she looked at her son in the rear view mirror.

"Okay…Ali and I were remembering Christmas's past, in the olden days, before they started handing out electric candles to everyone."

"The olden days," Sharon asked, "how 'olden'?

"Oh, probably about…eight years ago." Ty answered.

"Yah, yah, that's not the olden days." Sharon said, "But, anyway, go on."

"Well, back then, like I said, they gave everyone real candles. Even the kids got them if their parents said it was okay. Ali was about five or six and I was four…or somewhere around that age, we were just kids. Anyway, when the service was ending, someone came to the end of the aisle and would light a candle and then everyone would pass the flame onto the next person until all the candles in the church were lit."

"And after all of the candles had been lit and the lights were turned off, everyone would sing 'Silent Night'." Ali added to the story. "There I was, singing my little heart out, and Ty decided to get a better look at my face, so he moved his candle right in front of my nose. And the next thing I knew, my bangs were *melting*!"

"And, boy, do melting bangs ever stink! P.U!" Ty said as he broke out into laughter once again.

"Poor Matt, his eyes grew to the size of saucers and I'm sure that mine did too, but I had the presence of mind to reach over and cover Ali's bangs with my hand, while Matt snuffed out Ty's candle as he snatched it from his hand!"

"So, you two are probably the reason that we have to use electric candles, I bet!" Sharon said between bouts of laughter.

"Nah, it happened to other kids, too. We weren't the first."

"And we definitely weren't the last." Ali added.

"I don't think that liability insurance for churches will cover Christmas Eve candlelight services any more, unless the candles are electric. Thank goodness! It's a lot easier on the parents that way!" Jamie said, as she pushed the button on the electric door opener and began pulling into the garage.

"I'm so glad that we're finally home, Ty said, "I'm *really* ready to eat!"

Chapter Thirty-five

As Jamie stood before the clothes that had been squeezed into the small closet that she and Alison shared, she was having a hard time deciding what to wear on this sunny Christmas morning. She couldn't even remember last year's Christmas morning; let alone what she had worn; she assumed that it had probably been her pajamas.

In years past, they had always worn the new pajamas that everyone had opened after coming home from church on Christmas Eve. One gift had been the rule and it had always been the new, matching sets of goofy looking pajamas. She had gotten both Ali and Ty pajamas again this year. She had decided that some traditions needed to change, so she hadn't bought herself any pajamas and Ali and Ty's pajamas weren't matching. Ty's were a pair of more masculine camo pajamas and she had chosen a pair of pajamas with Eeyore's face plastered all over them, for Alison.

Jamie couldn't help but sigh when she thought about the fact that her children were going to rapidly become young adults, in the seeming 'blink of an eye'. She felt so proud of the wonderful persons that they were growing in to, wishing once again that their dad was here to see them grow. She had continued to worry about Alison, and how losing Lucy had been so devastating. She had even felt a little angry that Travis and his parents couldn't have let them keep Lucy until after Christmas. Yet, even as she had pondered that scenario, she knew that with every passing day, it would have been that much harder to let go of their little black companion.

As she thought over everything that she and Travis had discussed on the morning when they had met, Jamie had been in complete agreement to let Lucy go as quickly as possible. She had continued to second guess herself in the days following, wondering if she had made the right decision. No matter what, the decision had been made. She was grateful that Travis and his parents would be coming here this afternoon and that Lucy would be staying for the rest of the week. As much as Ali and Ty didn't want just visitation, she was thankful that Lucy wasn't going to be completely gone from their lives. Jamie, too, had wished that things had turned out differently, as she'd realized how much she had come to love having the little dog to keep her company on the days when the kids weren't around.

She sighed again, before resuming her hunt for the right outfit, finally settling on a pair of black slacks and a royal blue sweater. It was the one that Matt had bought her for Christmas a couple of years ago. He'd said that he had chosen that particular color of blue, to match her eyes. *Oh, Matt, how I wish that you were still here.*

As Jamie slipped the sweater over her head, she was thankful that it hadn't made a complete mess of her hair, as Alison entered the room wearing her 'ho-hum' Eeyore pajamas.

"Mom, I've got a fresh pot of coffee brewing to go with your traditional Christmas morning cinnamon rolls. I can never decide what I like most about Christmas morning, especially now that I'm getting *older*...opening gifts, or the cinnamon rolls and hot chocolates that we always have while we're opening up our gifts."

"Thank you, Ali." Jamie said, giving her daughter a quick hug. "Please let your brother know that I'll be down shortly and that as soon as Sharon arrives, he can tear into the remaining gifts under the tree while the rest of us take time to enjoy opening our gifts, as we *slowly* munch on our rolls!"

"Yah, and he's going to eat his rolls like he opens his gifts...in record time!" Ali replied, returning her mother's hug, as they heard the doorbell ring.

"And that would be Sharon." Ali said as she headed down the stairs, to let their friend in for the day's celebration.

"So, what time does the little black princess arrive today?" Sharon asked as she helped Jamie pick up the remainder of the wrapping paper from the gifts that they had all exchanged, while the kids headed up the stairs to change out of their pajamas.

"They're going to bring her over early this afternoon. That way we can all meet and get to know one another." Jamie replied as she stuffed the paper and ribbons into the kitchen trash can. "I'm so glad that you're going to be here when they come, Sharon. But, I do have just one question for you; do you think that you can get your reindeer in check by turning off his blinking nose before they arrive?"

"Ha, ha. And, yes, I'll turn his nose off well before they arrive. Why? You don't think that a lawyer and his parents will approve of a very colorful and welcoming sweater?"

"Actually, Sharon, I was only kidding. I think you should let Rudolph blink away while they're here. If they can't accept your blinking reindeer, well, I think that will be a pretty good way to judge their characters. Don't you agree?" Jamie asked with a giggle.

"Amen, sister! Hopefully his batteries won't run out of juice before they arrive! And now, what do you want me to do next, to get the rest of this show on the road?"

"If you wouldn't mind taking a peek at the turkey for me, that would be great. I would *love* to have dinner turn out just right this year. I think that we had Hamburger Helper for Christmas last year, thanks to Ali and Ty. If it had been left up to me, we probably would have just eaten peanut butter and jelly sandwiches!"

"Jamie, it's been so nice to hear you joking around and to see you smile so much, once again. In the last few months, I feel like I've gotten my 'old' friend back again."

"Oh Sharon, I couldn't have done any of the past year without you at my side. You're an example of what a true friend really is. And I'm learning that when it comes to grieving, time, truly, is a friend. As each day continues to subtly pass by, the pain begins to lessen. There's still a huge hole in all of our hearts, but time has been doing its work in helping us to heal. Time, together with the love and prayers of so many friends, especially friends like you."

This time it was Sharon who wiped a tear from her eye as she watched Jamie head up the stairs to answer Alison's request for her Mom's opinion on what to wear.

"I'll get it! Alison! I think they're here with Lucy!" Ty said, hopping off the stool at the breakfast bar and cupping his hands to yell up the stairs for his sister.

He had no sooner opened the front door when Lucy came yipping into the entryway, allowing him to give her a quick pet before she ran rapidly up the stairs to see if Alison was anywhere to be found.

"Hello again, Tyler." Travis said, reaching to grasp the youngster's hand.

"Everyone just calls me Ty and I'd really like it if you wanted to call me that, too."

"Ty it is, then." Travis replied as he stepped aside to introduce the young man to his parents. "Mom, Dad, this is Ty…Jamie's son."

"It's nice to meet you, young man." Travis's mom said with a smile as her husband reached around her to shake Ty's hand.

"And, I'm Alison, Ty's sister." Ali said, as she and Lucy appeared at the top of the stairway leading up to the living room. "Please come in. My mom and her friend, Sharon, will be down in just a few minutes."

Ty led the way up the stairs from the entry and even had the presence of mind to offer them something to drink while they waited.

"Thanks, Ty, but we won't be staying very long. We don't want to impose on your day any more than we already are." Travis answered as he and his parents settled onto the couch.

As Jamie descended the steps from the bedrooms upstairs, Travis had to stifle a gasp as he noticed how beautiful she looked in a sweater that matched her eyes. He was so thankful that he hadn't accidentally slipped and said "wow" or worse yet, whistled. Coming down the stairs behind her was a woman whose sweater had a huge reindeer with a nose that was blinking bright enough to light up the room.

Travis and his father both stood, as Jamie and Sharon came walking into the living room.

"Hi, I'm Jamie, and this is my best friend, Sharon…and her friend, Rudolph." Jamie said with a smile that lit up the room every bit as much as did the reindeer's nose.

Travis's dad laughed, as he reached out to take the young woman's hand in his and then quickly turned to do the same, shaking hands with Sharon, also.

"My name's Dave and this is my lovely bride, Mary." He said, as he turned to smile at his wife, before adding, "Well dear, it seems that you're not the only one who owns a blinking reindeer sweater!"

Mary began to laugh.

"Don't tell me that you own a sweater like *this*?" Sharon asked incredulously.

"Oh yes, I do. One of the things that I like best about Christmas, are the bargains after it's all over! Especially the Christmas sweaters; they're one of my weaknesses!"

"I can vouch for that." Travis said, smiling down at his mother. "She could easily win every ugly sweater contest around, with the variety that she has hanging in her closet."

After his mother jabbed him in the ribs with her elbow, the ice was broken as they all began to laugh.

An hour later, as Travis and his parents prepared to leave, it felt as if they had all become friends in the short amount of time they'd shared. The kids had delighted Travis's mother with their stories of school and friends and Sharon had helped to keep everyone laughing with all of her crazy stories of her many adventures in the classroom. Jamie and Travis had easily talked when they slipped into the kitchen to get drinks and a plate of Christmas cookies that Jamie had finally talked everyone into having.

As Jamie and Sharon carried the empty plates and cups back to the kitchen, Sharon nudged Jamie and whispered, "Invite them back for dinner."

"Don't you think that would be a little awkward?"

"Jamie, I overheard Mary tell Alison that they're going to go and get something to eat after they leave here...I'm assuming that she meant at a restaurant. It's Christmas. No one should have to eat restaurant food on *Christmas*." Sharon urged.

"Fine then, I'll ask them," Jamie whispered, glad that the kids and Lucy had the attention of their guests, "But, I doubt that they'll accept."

"I'll work my magic and I bet they will." Came Sharon's whispered reply.

"Whew, that was a lot harder than I thought it would be!" Sharon said after Travis and his parents had gone out the door, promising to return for dinner in a few hours. "I'm so glad that I realized Travis's hesitation was because he didn't want to leave his dog alone for too long. As soon as I told him that his dog would be welcome, too, he relaxed a little. Isn't that sweet, a good looking single guy who doesn't want to leave his dog alone on Christmas? I hope it's okay that he's bringing a dog with him."

"No, that's perfectly fine. After living in a kennel and a rescue, I'm sure Lucy won't have a problem with another strange dog. Hopefully, it's not a Saint Bernard! And, you're right, it's Christmas and I'm glad that the three of them will have us to share it with. Especially since Mary seems to have the same taste in clothes as you do!" Jamie said as she put the topping onto her sweet potato soufflé before returning it to the oven

"I know...hard to believe, huh? A refined, older woman with taste like mine! That doesn't bode well for me as I approach old age! And Jamie...I couldn't help but notice how Travis was looking at you the entire time they were here."

"Oh no. No, Sharon. I'm not interested in anyone...not after what Matt and I shared. I never want to fall in love again and open myself up to being hurt if anything ever happened to them. And, no one could ever measure up to the love I shared with Matt."

"Good grief, Jamie, I don't want you to marry the guy...I just said that he had a hard time taking his eyes off of you while they were here." Sharon said with a wink.

"I know you too well, my friend. You're a romantic through and through. Don't think romance…think friendship…and joint custody of a little black dog! And that's joint custody with his parents, not him!"

"Okay, okay. I'm thinking 'just' friendship at your request. Now, let me check out that pumpkin pie I brought. Since I'm rather good at burning things, I'd prefer not to do so this time. I'd like to make a good impression, for a change." Sharon said as she turned the reindeer's blinking nose back on.

Chapter Thirty-six

"What was I thinking when I asked three additional people to come back to share dinner with us? This place is way too small. As it is, I only have a tiny table!"

"Jamie, it's going to be fine. Ty and I just picked up my card table and if we put the two of them together, there will be plenty of room for all of us to sit down…and see…Ty moved the sofa back against the wall and the tables fit just fine! And we can serve everything buffet style. Set the food out on the kitchen counter. Now that I've sliced the turkey and put it in a cake pan, it can sit on the stove to stay warm and the pie and cookies can go on the breakfast bar. Everything is going to be just fine, so stop stressing!" Sharon encouraged.

"Unless they walk in with a Saint Bernard!"

"Seriously, Jamie, do you really think he'd bring a great big dog to a stranger's home for Christmas. If I hadn't interrupted him when he started talking about his dog, maybe he could have mentioned what kind it was…but you know me…I leap before I look!"

Jamie broke into unabated laughter as she looked around at the cramped space, trying to imagine how they would ever have room to get by one another while dishing up their food.

"What? What's so funny?" Sharon asked with a puzzled look on her face.

"I'm just having visions that are dancing around in my head, and believe me; they definitely are not of sugarplums! They're of me, pouring food down the front of one of our guests!"

"It won't be you, Jamie! It will be me, your good friend Sharon, the queen of disasters. Just you wait and see!"

As she and Jamie broke into uproarious laughter, bringing Ali, Ty and Lucy into the kitchen to see what was happening, the doorbell rang.

As Alison opened the door, Mary came into the house, carrying food containers and a couple of gift bags.

"Travis and David will be right in; they're getting the dog out of the car and going to let him take a little time to relieve himself." Mary said as she handed the gift bags to Alison. "Do you mind setting these up under the tree, dear?"

"No, not at all." Ali replied. As she headed up the stairs, she couldn't help but wonder who the gifts were for, and where on earth they had gotten anything on Christmas Day?

"Travis will probably have to carry his dog up the stairs; it's older and since it's been running circles with Lucy for the past week, he seems to have developed a little limp." Mary said as she followed Ali up the stairs. "Travis won't want him to strain his leg."

"There are cookies and some of my home made pizelle cookies in the containers. I'm just sorry I didn't have more to contribute for your gracious invitation to dinner." Mary said as she walked into the kitchen, where Jamie and Sharon were putting the finishing touch on the side dishes.

"Mary, you didn't need to bring anything. We're all just so glad that you accepted the invitation to join us."

"That goes ditto for me." Sharon interjected, as she watched Mary remove her coat and hand it to Ty, after his offer to take it from her. "Oh, wow! And I see that you went home and put on one of your Christmas sweaters!"

"Well Sharon, I figured that if you were going to be blinking at the table, I could wear my sparkling elf sweater! I don't get a lot of occasions when I can wear something like this. David and Travis would be horrified if I ever showed up at one of their office parties dressed in one of these!"

"Just like two peas in a pod, don't you think, Jamie?" Sharon asked as she stepped next to Mary and draped an arm over her shoulders.

They all broke into laughter, being joined by Lucy, who added a few of her own high pitched barks, just before Ty scooped her up into his arms.

"Merry Christmas!" They heard Travis and his dad both say, as they came through the front door.

"I hope it's okay that we just walked in without knocking again." Travis said as he came up the stairs behind David, who carried additional gift bags.

Travis was just about to set Rascal onto the floor when Alison screamed and ran to gather the little blonde dog into her arms.

"Rascal…is *your* dog?" she asked, as the tears began to run down her face.

"I thought you might recognize him as one of Susan's rescue dogs. I didn't realize that it would make for such a tearful reunion, though." Travis said, as he swallowed the lump in his throat, caused by the touching scene before him.

Ty held tightly onto Lucy, who had taken one look at the other dog in Ali's arms and began to excitedly bark and carry on. Ty quickly stepped closer and was amazed as he watched Lucy lean toward Rascal so she could give his fuzzy face a kiss, while Rascal turned away from Lucy to smother Ali's face with kisses of his own.

"Oh my goodness…this is the most amazing Christmas ever!" Jamie said as she watched the joy on her children's faces. "Lucy and Rascal were best dog friends! Ali is the one who taught him some of the signs that he knows! I can't believe that you were the one to adopt Rascal!"

"Didn't Susan tell you who adopted him?" Travis turned to Jamie, looking confused.

"Ali learned about his adoption, but she hadn't been at the shelter for a little while, and Susan was gone when she went in on Friday and Saturday. Jessica, one of the regulars was out, too, so no one knew much of anything about Rascal. As a result, Ali hadn't gotten any of the information about his adoptive family. We might need to do a little more negotiating for some additional visitation rights! Ali had desperately wanted to bring both of them home, but we just couldn't accommodate two dogs in this small place."

"Mom, can you believe this?" Alison asked as she walked in to the kitchen. "I can't believe what a wonderful Christmas this is turning out to be!"

"Not just for you, but for us, also." David said, as he set the additional gift bags onto the floor near the tree. "It's been awhile since we've had anyone to spend Christmas with, other than just Travis."

"Gee, thanks, Dad. I always thought that 'just Travis' was good enough."

"You know what your Dad means, Travis. You *are* good enough, but you have to admit that this is a lovely way to be able to spend Christmas, don't you?"

"I know exactly what you mean, Mom, and it's fine. I still love you both, despite what Dad just said." Travis said with a smirk as he placed a kiss on his mother's forehead.

"And on that touching note, I think that everything's ready so that we can all begin to dish up our plates." Jamie announced, as she set the final dish onto the kitchen counter.

"This meal was absolutely amazing. My thanks go to both you and Sharon for such delicious food." David said as he folded his napkin and set it next to his plate.

"I have to whole heartedly agree," Added Travis, "and I am so appreciative of such a good, home cooked meal."

"This really beats going out to eat for dinner. I used to cook, especially for special occasions like Christmas, but I've gotten a little lazy in my old age." Mary added with a smile.

"I prefer to think of it as 'advanced age', not 'old age'." David said as he smiled at his wife.

"Fine, David. Advanced age it is, then." She retorted with a laugh. "And Jamie, what would you like us to do, in order to help you tidy up?"

"Absolutely nothing." Sharon replied, on Jamie's behalf and hers. "Jamie and I have everything stacked in the sink and in the past, after the company leaves, the two of us always work together and we're able to get everything back in order in no time at all."

"Are you sure?" Mary asked. "I feel funny about leaving you with a mess."

"I'm sure, my kitchen is so small that it can barely support two people doing clean up." Jamie replied. "Sharon and I have developed a system over the years and we get everything done just as she said, in no time at all."

"We probably should be going soon." Travis spoke up. "But before we do, Dad, Mom and I have some gifts for all of you and we'd love to give them to you now, if that's okay?"

"Travis, you really didn't need to bring gifts. We hardly know you and gifts aren't necessary."

"We know that, Jamie, but after we left here, we discussed everything and I think that you'll be able to appreciate some of the gifts that we've decided to give to you. Ali or Ty, would you mind getting the gift bags out from under the tree?"

"I can do it." Ty volunteered.

"Go for it, Bro." His sister replied.

"Here's one for…Sharon." Ty said, as he delivered a large, colorful bag. "And this one is for Ali. Here's one for you, Mom. And…here's one for me!"

As soon as everyone had sat down, Travis turned to Ali and asked her to open her gift first.

After pulling the tissue paper out of the bag, Ali saw an envelope nestled in the bottom. She slowly removed it and looked to Travis before opening it.

"Go ahead, Ali, open the envelope and read what it says."

"To Alison, from the Redman Family, Your gift is a small black dog, named Lucy." Ali tried hard to swallow the lump in her throat and quickly wiped at the tears running down her cheeks, before continuing. "While the will is very specific about everything that John left behind, Lucy was his priority. We had made a gentlemen's promise to provide Lucy with a loving home. The will does not specifically say that it has to be our home; it just requested that we make sure that she would get to live out the rest of her life in a loving home. After meeting you and your family, we know that she will get all the love and care that John had desired for her to receive. Lucy is yours to keep; however, we do hope that you will allow us visitation. Merry Christmas, Alison, From David, Mary and Travis Redman."

When Alison finished reading the letter, there wasn't a single dry eye in the room. Even Ty, attempting to be the man of the family had been unable to hold back his tears. Alison held Lucy tightly to her chest, as she sobbed into the little dog's furry neck. When she finally looked up into the faces of those surrounding her, she softly said, "Thank you. This is one of the best Christmas's I've had, especially since my Daddy had to leave us."

Jamie rose from her seat to sit beside her daughter as the two of them held tightly to one another.

Mary wiped away her tears before turning to Sharon. "Why don't you go next? I think that we could all use a little laughter."

Sharon pulled the tissue paper from her bag and squealed as she pulled another colorful Christmas sweater from the bag. "I love it! Where on earth did you ever find something so unique?"

"When you take a better look, I think you'll be able to figure it out. I was so enthralled when I found it, I couldn't resist buying two of them, never knowing what I'd do with the second one…hold it up, Sharon, so everyone can see."

Sharon stood and held the sweater in front of her to give everyone a good view. Covering the front of the sweater was a picture of all the presidents' heads that were routinely seen on the face of Mt. Rushmore. Each president wore a Santa hat, except for President Roosevelt, whose head sported reindeer antlers. Mary stood up and reached inside the collar to turn the hidden switch to the 'on' position. Immediately, the antlers lit up, along with the balls on the Santa hats, as the song, 'White Christmas' began to play.

"What a hoot! I can't wait to show this one to my students! They're going to go wild, don't you think, Jamie?"

"You'd better believe it, Girlfriend. And the rest of the staff are going to be very impressed too, especially the History teachers!"

As they all burst into laughter, Jamie realized that this was going to be a Christmas that wouldn't easily be forgotten.

"Ty, you're next, if you don't mind." Travis said, turning his way.

It took only moments for Ty to tear the tissue paper out of the bag, revealing season tickets to the remaining pro-hockey games that were going to be played locally. "Are you kidding me? I absolutely love hockey...I used to play, back when Dad was still around."

"I know, I remember you mentioning that to me the day we met. I hope it's okay that I got two sets of tickets; I thought that maybe you and I could go together, if it's okay with your Mom."

"Absolutely." Jamie said as she watched Ty turn to look at her. "Travis, you have all really been much too generous. How can we ever thank you?"

"By opening your gift next." Travis said with a wink and a smile.

"Hmmm...it looks like...an envelope...with a letter inside." As Jamie removed the folded paper from the envelope, she noticed how official it looked and gasped as she began to read what was written.

"What? Travis, this can't be true. They always say that if it sounds too good to be true, it's because it usually is..." As Jamie continued to scan the page, she stopped to look into the faces of the people who had been complete strangers, until today. "No, there's no way that I can accept this...No...I..."

"Jamie, please listen to what I have to say," David said as he rose from the sofa to go and stand beside the young woman whose face registered complete confusion.

"But, no...this is...this can't be..."

"What?" Sharon's patience had worn completely thin. "What on earth are you stuttering about? Jamie, you know me...I can't stand being left in suspense!"

Forgetting the fact that there was a room full of people, Jamie turned towards her best friend with a complete look of shock, still unable to answer the question that was being asked of her. She handed the page to her friend, who quickly began to skim what had been written.

"Sharon, Jamie is just a bit confused right now. You see, she's just learned that she is going to be the recipient of a large home and an even larger sum of money." David paused before continuing. "John was my best friend, and he was also a very wealthy man who had decided to leave his home and a sizeable sum of money to his second most faithful companion, Lucy. She was the one who helped him to continue on after he lost his wife, many years ago. Lucy was even there at his side when he left his home for the final time. He had made well thought out preparations, because he wanted to be sure that if anything ever happened to him, Lucy would be well provided for."

Now it was not only Jamie who sat silently with her mouth hanging open, she had been joined by her best friend, who wore the same stunned look on her face. And for once in her life, Sharon was speechless.

"But, Travis, this is an unbelievable sum of money that we're talking about and a house located in *that* neighborhood has to be worth a fortune. There is no way that I can accept this gift from you and your parents!" Jamie spoke after finally regaining her composure.

"I can't think of a more deserving family." Travis spoke softly, "You won't have to sort through all of this alone. Dad and I will be here to help you with everything. If your family hadn't come along, Lucy might not be here at all. It was Ali who helped to rescue her from a shelter that was going to destroy her if she hadn't been adopted in time…and the Misfit Rescue took her in until Ali, and you, and Ty, gave her a home."

David cleared his throat before adding, "And if Mary and I had kept Lucy, we were going to be donating everything from her inheritance to the charities that John loved most. We were never going to keep Lucy's inheritance; we have no need of it. So this isn't really from any of *us*. It all belongs to Lucy."

"Dad's exactly right, Jamie. You were the ones who rescued Lucy. When you opened your hearts to a broken hearted little black dog, you had no idea that you were rescuing a little animal that had meant the world to a man who had made this little dog his world.

This inheritance isn't from any of us, Jamie, it doesn't belong to us. This is Lucy's gift…and it's from her, to all of you."

Epilogue

(1 year later…)

"Hi Travis. Wow, you look nice in a tux! And that's really saying something, especially since I'm a guy. Oh my gosh, and you and Rascal are wearing matching ties!" Ty said as he bent down to scratch the ears of the little dog who was sitting patiently beside his master.

"Hey Ty, you're looking pretty dapper yourself." Travis smiled as he looked into the face of the young man who had grown so much in the past year, that he was almost tall enough to look him in the eye.

"Come on in, Mom's almost ready for the big day. And I think that Ali is, too."

As Travis stepped into the foyer of their home, he was impressed by the tasteful decorating that had been done by Jamie, knowing that Sharon's input had been invaluable. He hadn't really been surprised when Jamie had made the decision to sell John's house and purchase something else. She had felt like it was too large and opulent for her family of three…four if you counted Lucy. She had taken many months before making any decisions at all, regarding the inheritance that had become hers to manage, on behalf of Lucy.

All of her decisions had been so well thought out that she hadn't required much help from either David or Travis. Before moving forward with any of the decisions that she'd made, she had welcomed their professional opinions, unwilling to move forward without their approval. Out of respect, they had only given minimal direction and input, trying to make sure that they hadn't placed any undue pressure on Jamie to change directions with any of her plans. Both Travis and his dad had been won over by the astute decisions that she had continued to make.

Even this house that she and the kids had chosen had helped to demonstrate a good sense of judgement that came naturally to her. She had chosen something, adequate in size, to meet the needs of her family, as her children continued to grow and mature into young adults. The home was a two story with a large kitchen and family room, for entertaining the many young people who were always welcome in their home. Not only did the house accommodate the young people, but it also had a yard that was welcoming to their friends and their pets.

The entire place had been furnished in simple, but tasteful furniture that was able to withstand the wear and tear of teenagers and dogs. And an occasional cat, Tigger being the primary one. Ali had continued to be an influence for adoption among many of her friends whenever they had expressed an interest in owning a pet and the new adoptees were always welcome in their home.

As Travis and Rascal followed Ty into the family room, Rascal immediately went over to lie on the bed that he claimed as his own whenever he came to spend time with his 'other' family. He immediately began to paw at the blanket that Alison had sewn for him, bunching it into a wad, for him to lay his head on.

"Well then, Rascal, why don't you just make yourself right at home!" Travis said as he smiled at his little dog, knowing that he hadn't heard a single word that he'd just said.

"He does that all the time. It's kind of funny, Ali will lay his blanket neatly on his bed and as soon as he sees it that way, he immediately goes over and bunches it up into a ball so he can use it for a pillow. He's a strange little dog."

"Yes, he is." Travis agreed as he smiled at his four legged companion.

"I think I'll go and see when Mom and Ali will be down."

"Sounds good, Ty. Thanks." Travis said as he leaned back onto the sofa and rested his head.

As he sat, eyes closed, he patted the small box that was tucked into his inside lapel pocket as he pondered all that had taken place in the past year. Both Lucy and Rascal had settled into their respective families nicely. Travis's parents loved the arrangements that had been set in place. Not only did they spend time with Lucy, but they had also had an opportunity to build a good relationship with Ty and Alison. The kids were rapidly becoming like the grandchildren that they had never had, as David and Mary spent time taking them out to movies and dinner, never missing any of the kids' school events or any of Ty's football or hockey games. At times, they had all been joined by Matt's parents, who were following through with their promise to play a more active role in the lives of their grandchildren, in honor of their son. All of them had begun forming close friendships with each other and when everyone was together, it felt like one big family gathering.

Lucy and Rascal had plenty of time together and were well adjusted to spending the night, off and on, between at all three homes. Both dogs seemed to have overcome their abandonment issues. Rascal's silly little personality had fully emerged, endearing him to everyone around him. Lucy was always meeting new people because of her outgoing personality, and Mary had begun taking her to one of the nursing homes, weekly. David could often be seen walking both dogs around the neighborhood as he enjoyed their companionship, without having the full commitment of owning a pet.

Travis and Jamie had slowly begun to spend time together. At first, it was primarily focused around the dogs and the kids. As time had passed, she and Sharon had begun to accept his invitations to go out to dinner, and eventually, he and Jamie had found themselves eating by themselves when Sharon had to cancel at the last minute. *Bless you, Sharon!*

"They said they're almost ready." Ty announced, as he walked back into the family room, causing Travis to open his eyes and set his daydreaming aside.

When Jamie and Alison finally came down the stairs and walked into the room together, Travis let out a low whistle. As Lucy came yipping into the room behind them, she too, was all decked out in a cute little outfit of her own, in the same rose color as Alison's dress.

"Mom, you look beautiful. And you look nice, too, Ali."

"I fully agree." Travis said as he rose to his feet, "Like two belles at a ball! Three, if we count Lucy."

"Oh, stop." Jamie said as she walked over to Travis and gave him a quick hug. "Where are your folks? I thought that they'd be coming with you."

"They're going to meet us there. Mom said that she wanted to let the four…six…of us ride over together. She and Dad decided to just take their own car and she had called Sharon to let her know that they'd pick her up on the way." Travis said, returning Jamie's hug. "Have you talked to Susan? Is she already there, finishing up the final arrangements?"

"Ali had called her earlier this morning. Susan said that she and Jessica have everything under control, and that we have absolutely nothing to worry about. They've got it covered."

"Well, I guess we should probably get headed out so we don't hold things up. After all, we're the guests of honor." Travis said as he bowed and swept his arm toward the front door.

"I've got your coats; it's really nice out right now, but the forecasters said that there's a chance of snow later on this afternoon and evening." Ty said, as he walked back into the room, carrying both Jamie and Alison's coats.

"Wow, thanks, Ty, that's *really* using your head!" said Ali as her brother helped her into her coat, while sticking his tongue out at her. After Travis had taken Jamie's coat from Ty, he stood, holding it open for her to slip her arms inside.

As Travis drove through the gates of the property, the brick pillars on each side had been wrapped with ribbon and bows. As they continued up the long driveway, they saw that it had been alternately lined with pots of small evergreens and white poinsettias, each one decked out with large red bows. As they finally reached the front of the large brick structure, the pillars to the entryway had been wrapped in garlands of evergreens, lit with tiny white lights that had been woven throughout. With the mountains as a backdrop, the scene before them was breathtaking.

"Wow…" Jamie and Ali echoed one another.

"Can you believe that this is really happening today?" Ali asked, as she continued to take it all in. "I never would have dreamed…"

"Since there are already so many people here, I'd better get parked, so we can get this show on the road!" Travis said as he maneuvered his car into the space that had been left open for them, near the front door."

As the six of them came walking to the building's entrance together, everyone in the crowd had stepped back and begun to clap. Susan and Jessica stood together, smiling from ear to ear, pleased with all that they had done. A large ribbon, with an even larger bow in the center, was draped from one pillar to the one opposite, barring an entrance into the building. Off to the side was a large square object, covered up with a green tarp, and on the opposite side, was a table, hiding something beneath its sparkling red and white cloth.

In the center of the porch, just behind the ribbon, stood a podium with a microphone attached to it, where Susan stood motioning for Jamie and Alison to come forward. Travis walked over to stand beside his parents and Sharon, and smiled when he noticed Ty and Alison's grandparents standing across from them, wildly waving to get their attention. Beside them, stood Devon and his dad, with Parker sitting quietly at their feet.

As soon as Ali and Jamie, leading Lucy and Rascal, slipped under the ribbon to stand at the front, Susan stepped up to the podium and adjusted the microphone before tapping it to make sure that it was live.

"Dearly beloved, we are gathered here today…" as the crowd began to laugh, "I'm kidding, I'm kidding…I've just always wanted to say something like that. And, besides, I needed to break the ice because public speaking is not one of my strong points! Dogs, yes dogs, are definitely my strong points and they have been my calling for the past ten years." Susan said as she looked down at Lucy and

Rascal, who were both sitting, miraculously quiet, as if they knew that it wasn't their time to speak.

"Every year, approximately 6.5 million animals enter U.S. animal shelters, nationwide. Of all the animals that find themselves being surrendered, approximately 3.3 million of them are dogs and 3.2 million of them are cats. About 1.6 million of those animals don't find other homes and they eventually, their time runs out." (Web; ASPCA 2018)

The crowd was silent as everyone listened to the statistics that Susan had just shared, and she had paused before continuing on. "But the exciting news is that around 3.2 million of those animals are adopted every year!" She paused again, as everyone had begun to clap. "Half of the adoptees are dogs and the other half are cats. Another 710,000 cats and dogs end up being reunited with their families, the majority of those are dogs, and about 90,000 of them are cats." (Web; ASPCA 2018)

"Ten years ago, when I visited a shelter while looking for my missing dog, I was struck by how many of the animals were left behind, never finding a much needed home. As I began asking questions about some of the ones who weren't being adopted, it was often because of their advanced age, or some of them were simply so matted and neglected that they continued to be overlooked. I went home and thought about things for a short period of time, and within weeks, I made some changes to my home so that I could accommodate a couple of extra dogs. My first two dogs were Digger, an old Jack Russell terrier whose name fit him perfectly, despite being old! The other one was Ollie, a neglected Shih Tzu that cleaned up really well. I only fostered them for a short period of time, until I found a forever home for each of them. As time passed and I made more modifications to my home, I was able to take in more dogs. Eventually, I gave my 'mission' a name, and it became the Misfit Rescue Dogs. As I continued to desire to help many more dogs, I realized that I couldn't do it on my own, so I recruited additional foster homes and other volunteers to help me." Susan stopped, as her eyes began to be wet with moisture.

"And then, along came Jessica and Alison, two wonderful dog lovers and faithful helpers. After we added a number of additional volunteers who were willing to foster for me," she said, as she swept her arm toward the crowd on her left, "we were able to save even more of 'man's best friends'." As time passed, Lucy and Rascal, the little pups sitting at my feet, eventually came into our rescue. When Alison took Lucy home she had no idea at the time, that Lucy came with…well, I guess that one could say…baggage!" Susan stopped to laugh along with the others in attendance. "But it was *really good* baggage! We also had no idea how truly intertwined Lucy and Rascal's lives were going to be, nor did we have any idea that Lucy's 'baggage' would equate to being a rather large inheritance!" As Susan bent down to gather Lucy into her arms and set her onto the podium, Lucy leaned her face toward the microphone and barked, as the crowd broke into laughter.

"And now that she's put in her two cents worth, I'll continue…It is because of these two little abandoned dogs that we all stand here today. Lucy, at the encouragement of Rascal, I'm sure, has donated a portion of her inheritance for the purchase of this wonderful building and the property that it stands on. This will all adequately take care of the dogs that are currently in our care, with plenty of room to grow and the possibility of adding other animals. I could never have imagined that one day, this is where we would be and I continue to stand in awe of the wonderful gift that these dogs have all been given. So, without any further ado, Ty, will you and Travis step to my right, and get ready to pull off the tarp for me?" Susan waited as they stepped over into place on either side of the large tarped object, "I now present to you…" she said as the tarp was being removed, "L & R Misfit Animal Rescue!"

As the sign was revealed, the crowd began to cheer, whistle, and applaud.

"And now, we have one final thing to take care of. Jamie, will you take the covering off the table on my right?" The cloth was removed to reveal two very large pairs of golden scissors. After Jamie had lifted them off the table, she handed one pair to Jessica and the other pair to Ali.

"Girls, if you'll step on either side of the bow and set your scissors in place, we'll all count down from three and then, I want you each to snip the ribbon. Okay everybody, all together now…Three…two…one…" As the girls cut the ribbon and the bow dropped onto the cement porch, Susan said, "And the L & R Misfit Animal Rescue is now, officially open for business!"

When the crowd had finally begun to quiet, Susan set Lucy down and adjusted the mic once more. "Before everyone begins to wander around and explore our new facility, please enjoy the sandwiches and other refreshments that have been provided for all of you, in the foyer. Make sure you pay attention to the signs that have been set near the cookies and cakes, because some of them are for people and the others are for canines. But before we all go in, I'd like to ask Travis, Rascal and Jamie to all step forward."

Jamie looked at Travis with a puzzled look on her face as she approached the center of the building's entrance. After moving the podium off to the side, Travis came to stand beside her. When he looked down at Rascal, he asked, "So, old boy, are you ready to help me out?"

As Travis got down onto his knee next to Rascal, he fiddled with something on the collar, before pivoting to look up at Jamie. "Jamie…I know that you might still need some time, and you can take all the time that you want…but, I just have to ask…would you be willing to become Mrs. Travis Redman?" Travis paused, "Jamie, will you marry me?" he asked, as he showed her the ring that he had just removed from Rascal's collar.

As Jamie stood dumbfounded with her mouth hanging open, she was unable to speak. Ali and Ty made their way over to stand beside their mother and as each took one of her hands, she looked at them, seeing the happy approval in their faces. She was finally able to swallow the lump in her throat and find her voice. "Yes! Yes, Travis…we will *all* marry you…*and* Rascal! Ali, Ty, and Lucy! And me! Yes!" she said.

After rising onto his feet, Travis wrapped her in his arms and began to spin both of them around in a circle, as the crowd began to cheer and a gentle snow began to fall.

♥♥♥

In loving memory of my little dog, Rascal
Despite your low vision and deafness, I'm so glad that I brought you home.

I wasn't the one who did the rescuing; you and Lucy were the ones who rescued me.